SUCTION CUP DREAMS

Suction Cup Dreams

An Octopus Anthology

Edited by David Joseph Clarke

Obsolescent Press

Suction Cup Dreams

Illustrations by Natasha Aldred.

Additional graphical elements by Pelican Bishop.

Obsolescent Press

www.obsolescentpress.com

Publisher's Note:

ISBN: 978-0-9855013-5-8

First Edition

Permissions

Table of Contents

Introduction

Dr. Christine Huffard

The morning high tide sloshes against the limestone cliff, tosses me around, and I lose my spot. Was it there? No—there, next to that little rock with the Padina algae growing on its shoreward edge. When each wave recedes, the algae comes about to reveal the octopus's den entrance. Two pea-sized eyes bob up and down to avoid each sweep of the algae. A juvenile jackfish pauses overhead, but lacks the cues to trigger a hunt. When the coast is clear one pale arm lashes out and starts worming around nearby pebbles, bringing a select few closer to the hole. For the next four hours I float motionless, breathing on snorkel to watch this little octopus and record its daily goings on.

Today was as typical as it gets. Its eyes emerged shortly after dawn. When the tide was waist-deep, it pushed last night's sand out of its den. When the tide fell to knee-deep, it came out of its den, found food, avoided predators, and fought over a female (maybe next time buddy, when you're bigger). Half a dozen times today I looked up from my underwater note-taking and briefly lost track of my target. Half a dozen times I scanned for it among rocks, swaying clumps of different types of algae, a sea hare, a small conch, each one a component of the background the octopus tried to substitute for itself. Each time this happens, I'm reminded that my studies run counter to the essence of my subject. Is it possible to describe an animal that defies recognition, classification and pattern in order to survive, and spends its days in constant hope of being lost in a mirage?

Octopuses are defined more by exceptions than by norms. They are molluscs, but they are not shelled like their ancestors and many existing relatives. They can learn and remember, but they are invertebrates that never meet their parents and they do not appear to form what we think of as relationships. Many octopuses can express an enormous repertoire of visual signals, but communication to each other appears limited to a few basic sentences such as "I'm male", "I'm mature", and "I'm going to fight with you." Unaided by color vision, octopuses can change the color and texture of their skin to match the background. Their skin has evolved as predators eat the more conspicuous individuals, leaving the most cryptic to survive and reproduce. One of their most famous defenses, their ink, is deadly to themselves and known to elicit feeding behavior in their predators. Yet through both evolution in this world and mythological reputations we have created, this animal, so physically unlike us, has been bestowed exceptional qualities we otherwise consider signs of humanity—eyes that look like ours, the ability to walk, and a gifted brain. Each statistic we know of the octopus is countered by a greater weight of paradox.

The octopus's lack of its own identity and its brush with ours, allow it to effortlessly slip from fiction to non-fiction, a transition well captured in Suction Cup Dreams: An Octopus Anthology. Suction Cup Dreams is an impressionistic anthology, each story providing a unique and thought-provoking perspective of what it means to be, know, or be influenced by an octopus. True to the octopus that purposefully evades definition, the stories in Suction Cup Dreams stand free of archetypes, and evolve more from possibility than constraint. They do not demand your attention, but rather earn it through refreshingly unsaturated likenesses evocative of the octopus's tendencies. The characters face survival, consumption, and renewal entwined to a degree that is second nature to earth's softest cannibal. Like the octopus, the works in Suction Cup Dreams are not forced into intellectual boundaries or overt, preconceived themes, but rather are infused with subtle impulses, imaginative transformations, and just enough familiarity to make us question who the real chimera in these pages is.

Of Tentacles and Other Matters

It would probably come to a surprise to many people that octopi do not actually possess any tentacles. In modern scientific usage, only thin limbs with club-like appendages at their tips are considered tentacles whereas more thick limbs covered with suction cups are known as arms. While squid and cuttlefish still possess tentacles—two each—and nautiluses possess up to ninety suckerless tentacles, octopi possess eight arms. However, in common usage, people use the terms tentacle and arm interchangeably, so we have allowed authors to use either term as they deemed fit.

Another big debate is the proper plural form of octopus. There are many arguments over what is the proper way of describing a multitude of octopus creatures; the most common of them being octopuses, octopodes, and octopi. There are many good arguments for and against each of these, but since all three versions are legal in English, we have again left it up to the authors' discretion for their preferred usage.

— David Joseph Clarke

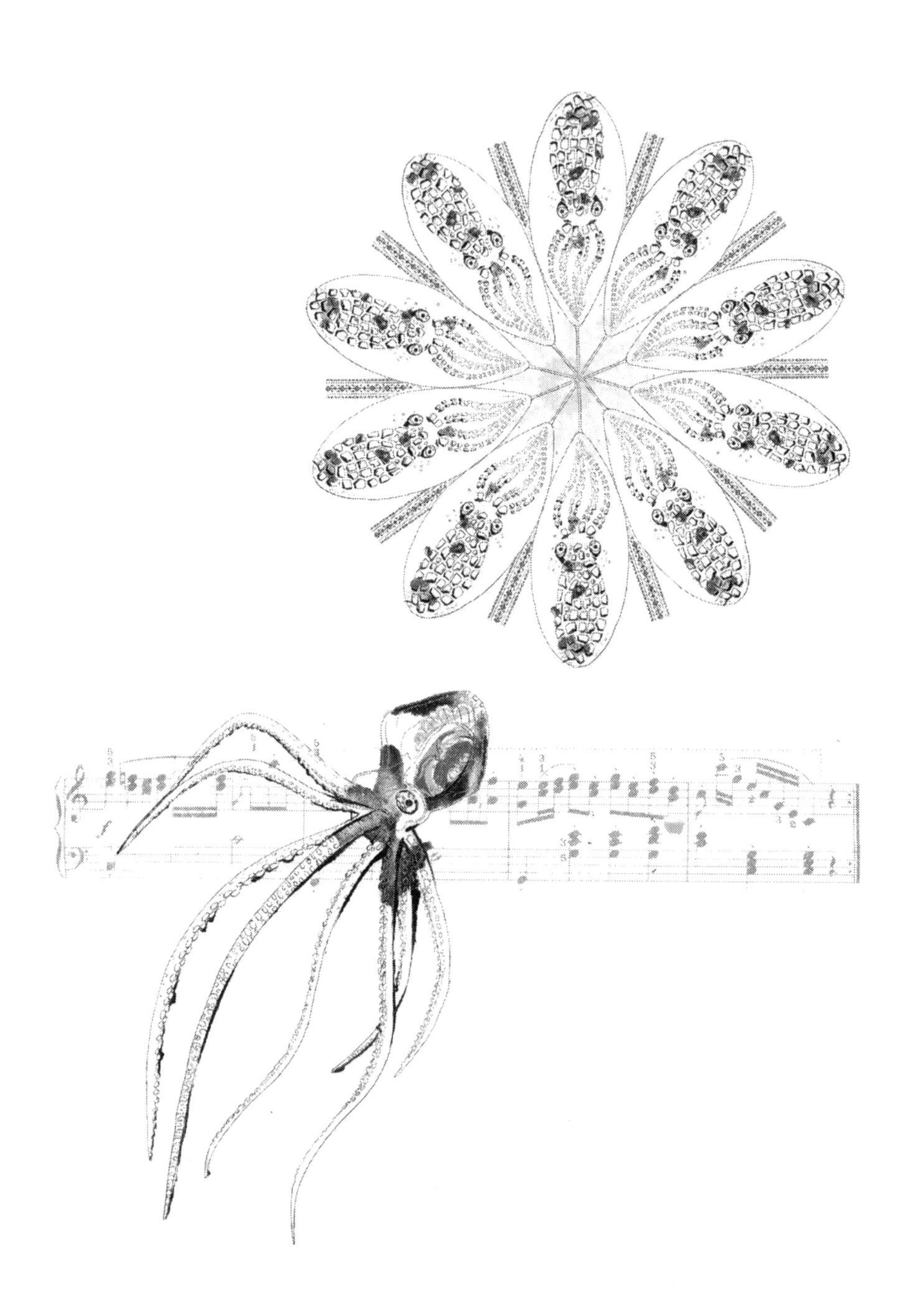

Reproduction

Jamie Lackey

The octopus strung her pearly white eggs on the cave roof one by one. They gleamed in the water-thinned light. Each one was precious. Her eggs. Her babies. Her future.

She stayed with them in the cave. She pushed water through her mantle to make sure each egg had enough to breathe. She checked them, one by one, over and over.

An eel slipped in through the narrow cave entrance, poked its long face into her nursery. She drove it off with ink and suckers and poison. But she knew it would come back.

She grew hungry, but she couldn't leave her eggs. She consumed one of her own tentacles, and felt stronger.

The eel lurked in the sheltered water outside of her cave. Driving it off again cost her another tentacle.

She kept the water moving, and she watched. The opaque shells grew transparent, and she could see her children inside. They wriggled, longing for freedom.

They were perfect.

One by one, they hatched. She watched them swimming away, out into darkness, into danger. Not one of them stayed, or looked back, or even hesitated.

The eel slithered past her cave toward her retreating babies. She was too weak to drive it away again, but she couldn't let it hurt her children. She latched onto it with her remaining tentacles. Its teeth raked at her, tore through her. Blood and ink darkened the water. She bit it again, and again. Its struggles weakened as hers did.

She sank to the cave floor with the empty eggshells, simply another spent casing.

Her babies rose toward the sun.

A Late Season Snow

T.E. Grau

He invited me to the ocean, to show me the octopi.

"Octopuses," he called them, but I knew what he meant, even if he didn't. They were in tide pools so shallow we could reach down and touch them, these slithering red rocks. I didn't even have time to put my makeup on before I was out the door. My parents never asked where I was going. They stopped asking years ago, much sooner than they should have.

The gray clouds threatened a late season snow, the last of the year before everything opened back up for spring. Snowfall, on a deserted beach, with a smiling boy holding my hand as the waves crashed all around us, leaching through blackened driftwood and echoing off the cliffs. This was fairy tale stuff from the books I read to myself as a child while my mother wept on the other side of the wall.

He was waiting for me down at the water's edge, pacing and smoking a cigarette next to a bottle resting on four stacked cinder blocks. Nervous, like all boys are right before their first time. Like all girls are every time. There was a raggedy old boat dragged onto the sand nearby. Did he paddle here like a Native Brave? I'd never been to his house. Couldn't even imagine what it would look like, other than a dirty couch and beer cans. Maybe he lived out on the overgrown pirate islands just off shore, which are supposed to be uninhabited but aren't really. Maybe he'd take us there in his boat, all skull and crossbones, and I'd finally be able to leave the weight of mainland behind.

I made my way down the steep cliff side, filling my sneakers with burrs while basking in the light of his sideways grin. My lips suddenly felt naked, craving a sheen of gloss. I kept my eyes low, wishing my lashes were a little heavier and much longer. He didn't bring a blanket, but I didn't care. Boys never think of things like that.

We'd never been around each other in a place so quiet, so we danced instead of talked, climbing on half buried tree trunks and mossy boulders, laughing at things that weren't even funny. Waltzing, waltzing, trying to keep time to the jagged beats coming from inside our ribs. I eyed the tide pools, dreaming of red octopi, hoping that he'd show me. I wanted him to teach me things that I didn't know. He just looked up at the road snaking around the top of the bluff. Round and round we twirled, never getting any closer.

Finally, he staggered away from me and collapsed to the ground, as if overwhelmed by it all, crossing his arms over his eyes. I knelt beside him and wrote our names in the wet sand. Before I could finish, he wrapped his hands around my waist and rolled me on top of him as if I didn't weigh a thing. I could feel my face flushing, but didn't have anywhere to hide. He brushed damp hair behind my ears and kissed me, devouring my anxious smile. He smelled like burnt menthol and peach schnapps. Like a smoldering orchard. He tasted good.

He pressed his hand against my cheek, caressing it awkwardly like they do in the movies, oil-stained fingers catching on the briny droplets misting my skin. His fingers were just as cold as my face, so I couldn't tell where I ended and he began. Then he reached down and looked for the warmer places of my body. I leaned into him, shivering from something more than the cold. He pulled up my shirt, peeling back my layers, but I stopped him. Not yet. The dance wasn't over. I took his hand and kissed his fingers and asked if he was going to show me the octopi. He laughed, teasing at first, then laughed again in that weird way that didn't include his eyes, realizing what I had said. The word I had used. The word he had used earlier. When we met, he accused me of being a stuck up smart girl. I giggled like an idiot and told him he was wrong. Just like he was wrong today. He knew what I was, even if I didn't. His smile disappeared, but I could see his mind still working. "Please?" I asked, remembering my manners.

He lunged at me, moving faster than I thought he could. Boys don't dance like girls do. I backed up, and told him that we need to go see the octopi. He told me it was time to see something else, and forced my hand down his baggy jeans. The top button was undone under his shirt, like he was ready the whole time. Before I even got to the beach. I pulled my hand back, disgusted. Not because of what I felt, but because of the way he wanted me to feel it. This wasn't how it was supposed to be. The snow hadn't fallen yet, like it was waiting. Holding it all in.

A hand grabbed my wrist. I tried to shove him back, but he was too strong. He clamped his mouth over mine, banging my teeth as the air left my lungs. He didn't taste good anymore. He tasted drunk. He stunk like my father. I pulled my head away and he bit my lip. I screamed and clawed at his face, taking a piece of him, as he lifted me up by my shoulders and slammed me back down, again and again until he pounded the sound out of me. There were large rocks buried in this sand, on this beach where no one came. I hit my head on one and my vision started to dim. He never held my hand like I thought he would, but the waves did crash around us, leeching through the blackened driftwood and echoing off the cliffs that drank my screams and didn't leave a drop.

* * *

I woke up an instant later with a flutter of eyelids that sounded like the wings of departing gulls, my back still heavy on the sand. I could feel the grit in my hair, gumming up the bleeding crack in my skull that now felt like a hollow space behind me. I wondered if the rock that broke me open now served as my pillow, but I couldn't move my head to find out. It was night now, and there was a faint glow in the darkness. The clouds must have cleared off without gifting the world with their promised late season snow. I gathered my strength to stand up, but my arms or legs wouldn't listen. They were tired, disappointed, and hoped the cold would protect me for now until something else came along. He was gone, retreating footprints looking no different than the abandoned dance steps, leaving me on the sand that held me down in his absence. Leaving me to the ocean that would soon rise and take me down inside while I stared up at the empty sky. My ears filled up. I smelled salt and rotting fish. Spilled liquor. I needed to regain my limbs and get out of there. He lied to me. He never showed me the octopi.

I fixed my watering eyes on the bright moon, smaller than I ever remembered it, shimmering and wrinkling like reflected in a pool. It seemed so far away. I felt weightless, sinking.

That's when the snow started to fall, backlit by lunar bluish white. It was the first time I had seen the very beginning of a snowfall. The snowflakes formed out of the shapeless dark and descended, as if created on command. They were large and fluffy and tumbled as they fell, enjoying the lazy, inevitable journey as much as I was.

A snowflake landed on me. Then another, and another. On my chest, on my forehead. On my cold hand that was never entwined in his, that wasn't strong enough when his was. The snowflakes didn't melt, but after a moment, they did begin to move. The grasping of delicate, intelligent tendrils, folding and attaching, finding sight with each suctioned grip. With great effort, I forced my eyes to look down and realized that these weren't snowflakes at all.

They were tiny octopi. Thousands of them. Translucent, eight-legged stars, refracting the moon and lighting up white like newly formed snow. They continued to fall softly on my skin, covering me in a gently collecting quilt of tiny legs and black, unblinking eyes.

Once they had gathered, they began to consume me, devouring my mushy flesh that dissolved into whirling particles like wet crackers in hot soup. A thaw spread through the brittle chill holding me together, and I imagined that I would smile if I could, knowing that I'd be carried away into the night inside countless baby octopi.

As my body was slowly absorbed, I realized that I had been looking not out of myself, but *at* myself the entire time. I could move now, floating above the rippled sand that danced with kelp, littered with reef and rock, patrolled by schools of saucer-eyed fish and darting creatures that fled from the moonlight. And there I lay, lashed with cheap rope to four cinder blocks crossing my body underneath the throbbing octopod mass like a ribbon on a birthday present, cocooned inside a wriggling shroud of hatchlings that chewed me up at the bottom of the sea.

I watched my own disintegration until what the world knew of me was gone, and what I would remain continued on. They slowly turned red, just like I had always dreamed.

He finally showed me the octopi.

Obey the Octopus

Joe Jablonski

1

The repetitive droning of an alarm clock brought John to consciousness.

He stretched long and loud before crawling out of bed, his mind and body locked in that eternal struggle between man and sleep. The itch on the top of his head was faint; the buzz, low and barely audible. He ignored both as he transversed the darkness of his third floor apartment with the ease of five years of familiarity.

The TV flickered in the other room. John listened with little interest as a light skinned, mustachioed gent blathered in a multi-regional drawl. Only the base details of the man's words registered: 25 year old male. Severe Anorexia. Self inflicted gunshot wound. Motive unclear.

Sucks for him, John thought as he entered the bathroom.

With the feel of cold linoleum beneath his feet, he turned on the light and screamed at what stared back in the mirror.

An octopus was leached to the top of his skull; bright yellow and aglow with pulsating blue rings. His eyes met the creatures' through reflections. The octopus' gaze bored into his very soul. The buzzing grew louder. Hypnotic. At that moment nothing else existed.

Fear turned to panic.

John ran to the kitchen trying to pull the six pound invertebrate from his dome, but the creature held strong, its tentacles suctioned tightly to his flesh.

His fists of fury didn't work.

A frying pan had even less effect.

The octopus remained unphased by all attempts, and for John, liberation seemed an unattainable goal.

The room throbbed in his peripherals as he dropped to his knees with arms aflailin', a foreign hunger bombarding his subconscious.

A knife gleamed bright from the counter. He reached out for it with an unsteady grip. Inches from the handle, a sudden pain struck his nervous system as the octopus lodged his beak into John's cerebral cortex, thick black ink seeping from the point of contact. Darkness was swift as his body collapsed with commands not his own.

Panic turned to surrender.

"That's a good boy."

* * *

By midday John was fetal on the floor, on the verge of suffocation, and in complete dejection. The octopus had now tripled in size. He could feel his own weight slowly withering away as the octopus fed on both body fat and silent misery alike.

Suddenly, there was a knock at the door. The octopus froze, its eight tentacles wrapped steady around John's face and neck.

"John, are you ok? You didn't show up to work." It was a soft female voice muffled by two inch thick wood. Laura, her name was

Laura. John could barely grasp the concept of her over the buzz of the octopus.

He didn't respond.

"John, come on, answer me."

Still nothing.

"Fine, I'm getting the landlord to open the door."

"No," John screamed louder than intended. He couldn't let anyone see him like this.

"John, open the fucking door. What's wrong with you?"

"Just leave already." He wanted more than anything to see her, but he knew she would never accept his octopussal affliction. He just needed time to think, needed time, needed...

"*Kill her,*" the buzz imparted on him. It didn't come with words, but sudden flashes of images and emotions. Something sonic cut through the cacophony and a brief flash of endorphin induced ecstasy washed through his system.

In a moment of weakness, John wanted to give in; to forever lose himself in the pure bliss gifted by the octopus.

"John, please," Laura pleaded.

A flood of foreign memories of him and Laura came back in rapid burst; intangible and barely coherent. He tried to hold on to them, but the octopus objected, and soon there was nothing left but murderous intention.

Through the door, Laura asked if there was a woman in there.

He yelled there wasn't, warring a disembodied hand as it reached for the door knob. He knew he needed to fight it...

She said he was scaring her.

He called her a bitch and said he never wanted to see her again. It took everything he had to form the words against the will of the octopus.

John waited a long minute, internally cringing at the things he was forced to say, praying he wouldn't have to say worse to get her to go away. Past the tears, past the tentacles slowly squeezing around his neck, the sound of heeled footsteps faded quickly down the corridor beyond.

Silence prevailed.

The octopus was not happy.

* * *

Sunset burned pastel through the apartments' single window, but John couldn't see it. A bulbous tentacle, stretched across his eyes, was suctioned to his exposed corneas. Blindness was the price of his previous disobedience. He could only perceive a distant glimmer of particles dancing through the dull haze of murky oblivion.

The octopus now covered the length of his combined head and torso, its tentacles completely enveloping his entire person. Underneath the plump mass, John existed as little more than a withered husk. He knew it wouldn't be long before he wasted away completely. At this moment, hopes of survival were nothing more than a forgotten memory.

The buzzing was now deafening. John ordered his limbs to claw away at his exposed temples; to rip the sound from his mind, but his muscles didn't obey.

For a split second through the connection, John sensed something subliminal from the parasitic growth. The creature seemed sedate, satisfied, full—complete.

Suddenly, he noticed something cold and metal in his grip. He fingered the length with what little movement he was allowed. First he felt the barrel, then the cylinder, then the hammer. Finally, the trigger.

Where'd the gun come from?

"*The octopus provides,*" said the buzz in his head.

Slowly, the buzz subsided and a slithering tentacle released its grip on John's arm. His nutritional value spent, John lifted gun to chin with a trembling fist.

"*Do it.*"

He never wanted not to do something so much in his entire life. In a final desperate attempt, he pushed back with his legs, and began thrashing wildly. He first slammed the octopus into the wall, then the corner of a table. The octopus squeezed tighter in response. John's already brittle bones cracked underneath the added pressure.

The buzzing was now ear-shattering. Through the agony, John could hear the cries of the collective multitude that had come before him, all their combined hopelessness and misery assaulting him at once.

John screamed until his lungs were depleted. Anger and pain were all he knew.

The beak drove in deeper, the pain of it excruciating. Overwhelming. A tentacle wrapped around his nose and mouth, cutting off both his screams and his ability to breathe. In seconds, his lungs turned to fire from the lack of oxygen.

It was all too much. Finally, not being able to take any more, John went still and gave into his fate.

The octopus was pleased.

"*Now!*"

He had no power to stop it; he no longer wanted to stop it. With the gun back to his head, he felt the subtle twitch of metal on metal friction as the trigger freed the hammer.

Suddenly, the buzzing was gone and one perfect moment of silent bliss followed.

It lasted a second.

It lasted an eternity.

The barrel flashed. John's lifeless body hit the floor with a quiet thump. The wall and ceiling were painted a chunky vermillion in the aftermath of .38 caliber death.

No sign of the octopus remained.

2

The repetitive droning of an alarm clock brought Blain to consciousness.

The itch on the top of his head was faint; the buzz, low and barely audible…

A Stranger Returns From An Unexpected Trip to the South China Sea

Henry W. Ulrich

It was early June when the young man walked into the town, only the sweat on his brow to cut the cruel, dry air flowing in the shadows of the San Bernadino range. He walked with a careful, measured pace down the pound-flat dirt track that lead to the center of the town, watching his feet eat up the miles of ground. The man smiled with the corner of his mouth at all the footprints; some half-obliterated by the scouring wind, others permanently embossed from so many repeated treads, almost all the leavings of prospectors that made up the dirt road's common custom. Several of the locals watched him, as he made his way on, in strange halting half-steps once he began to see which boot-prints his own feet fit into. They stared, though the young man's strange walk was the least of their reasons for it.

The saloon at the town's ragged epicenter of commerce was a watering hole for every new prospector to brag about his coming wealth in, and for every tired old hand to come and mourn his failed fortune. Rickety, squealing doors swung in easily at the young man's touch and he stood a moment to watch them in delight as they closed behind him, caterwauling in objection yet again. At first, no one cared about the young man, odd in grace and manner and unbroken sheen of sweat on his forehead. The prospectors in from fruitless stakes were too tired to pay much attention, and those few who had struck it lucky were too drunk to care. The gamblers were too busy losing it all in games of faro, or robbing easterners blind in crooked games of poker, and the young man might have stood there watching them forever if one of the bar girls hadn't looked over with a sigh.

"Why don't ya sit down and stay a while, mister, if you're looking to have a drink? You're making me nervous, just standing there—..." The girl, one Sallie Anne Mayfield, was a hardened one-year-veteran of all the unmannerly, rude, and just plain strange sorts that came through the swinging doors of the nameless saloon, and yet her mouth dropped open and her eyes widened as she stared at the figure.

"Jimmy? Jimmy Dougherty? James Dougherty?" Sallie's voice trembled, near breaking as she made her way towards him as though in a dream. "Jimmy—...but I heard...but you're here! You came back!"

The young man, now called Jimmy Dougherty (James Vogel Dougherty to his mother, one must assume), smiled again with delight as she came over to him, and then, after a silent moment where she stared at him and tried to keep from crying, caught her as she threw herself into his arms. She clung to him, desperately, looking up into his watery, blue eyes with confusion and need.

"You're clammy, Jimmy. Are you OK? How long have you been out along the mountain? We all thought—" And then, as she realized that all the dusty fellows off the fields, and the men with the slicked-backed hair and the marked carts, and the pock-marked fellows who smelled of burnt homesteads and hot iron were all watching them, she quailed and stepped back. “You shouldn’t be here alone, Jimmy, it just isn’t safe for you. I’m telling you—”

But the man called Jimmy Dougherty was just smiling, even as one of the big, ugly men came up from a table in the corner, with a Bowie knife in his hands and murder in his eyes, and even as the man lunged for Jimmy’s back, his hands were around the big bastard’s neck, squeezing and twisting. And he never stopped smiling at Sallie as he snapped the man’s neck like a frightened hare’s in the same moment he took the glinting blade into his hands to look over and marvel at. No one could quite agree which happened first, whether he wrested the knife away from the brute or slew him first, or if he (more impossibly still!) did each one-handed, but in the end he was still smiling at Sallie out of the corners of his mouth as he looked over the big knife.

“I’m back. I’m Jimmy Dougherty. It’s safe for you.”

And Sallie crushed him in her arms again, even as she tried not to think how strange and cool Jimmy was, and how odd the limp, dead body of his would-be killer was behind him on the ground.

* * *

The imposter had danced across the floor of the rich ocean on long, graceful arms for as long as living things could remember. He had no face, no firm form beyond the plastic twitching and surging of his body and form. He had made his desperate increase already, following the needful cries of his body to engender more, more! upon the fluid body of a female artist like himself. But that done, now there was only the change to draw him onward. One moment, a poisonous thing that no shark dare devour; the next, a flitting ray, to drive off a hungry beast in search of soft fare; the next, a long ribbon of a fish for the sheer joy of changing, of being. And then the strange, bright and hard things from the objects on the surface would descend into the rich ocean, and the imposter would break his performance for just a moment, soft supple arms investigating the curve of a round thing or the glistening sharpness of an edged thing, or once in a great while the yielding flesh of a dead thing.

And it was the passage of such a surface object, with the breathy cries of dismay and disgust of air animals, that would introduce another dead thing to the ocean world of the Imposter. His arms picked at the dead thing, the gleaming brightness that seemed to clip it together at its center, the hard things that dotted its body, having ended its life early many years before. And the Imposter grew to know the dead thing, to know all the decomposing truths of its strange, soft-around-hard-around-soft body, even to the strange things hidden in the wrinkled folds of its most curious organs. And, as was its joy, the Imposter changed.

The man they pulled from the water seemed a naif, at first; so eager to see them, to walk the deck, to live, but without words or understanding of what they spoke of. The first mate of the Aubrey Gale opined that perhaps the man has lost his wits from lack of air, as was known to happen. The ratings took turns guessing and then pointlessly betting on the rescued fellow's name, from the 'JD' brightly embossed on his belt buckle. The captain shook his head and joked with the mate about throwing their catch back, when finally the man spoke, as if trying out the words for the first time. "The fish is too strange, throw it back. The fish is too strange...don't throw it back?"

* * *

Ugly Ralph Sullivan ran from the saloon, onto the dirt road that ran out of town. He could feel the cheap leather of his boots threaten to give up, but Ugly Ralph didn't care. He didn't know if it was the man who he had seen in the saloon, or what that man did to Chuck Walgreen, or the whole situation which lit the fire under his feet, but Ugly Ralph just knew he had to run like the devil was after him. Because, as Ugly Ralph tried his best not to think, perhaps he was.

By the time he got to Ed Standing's camp, the stars were wheeling in the sky, and the gang gaped at his tale until Ed knocked him right onto his ass.

"Shut your mouth before you make more of a fool of yourself than you already have. Ok, you had a fright. Jimmy Dougherty isn't dead. He got Chuck. We thought we got rid of him in San Bernadino, but we didn't. It's that simple. He didn't go to the city sheriff, because we still have his claim and no one's come looking for us. He got lucky somehow, but now he wasted it. We'll do him again, for Chuck, and this time bury him in the ground." The men relaxed, and tried to laugh as Ed passed the good whisky around. Even Ralph wanted to,

despite the busted tooth and bruised ego that Ed left him with, but at the back of his mind the images of Jimmy's body as they bundled him away into the shipping crate kept playing. Those limp, sprawled limbs, the sticky, final pools of blood, the man's last desperate gasps. A body wasn't supposed to come back from that.

Ralph tried to drink to forget it, until Ed knocked three more of his teeth out for hogging the whisky.

* * *

It was almost like they had to teach their 'JD' how to be a man again. The first mate was adamant that the man would be an idiot for the rest of his days, at first, after he had to be re-taught how to drink from a mug and eat from a plate. But even when he was knocking over chairs in confusion, or repeating instructions for using the ship's head back to them for the third time, none of them could bring themselves to hold it against him. The weird little smile, and his willingness to keep trying to get living right made even the first mate keep at it, and after a week even he had to admit that JD was getting himself back. Eventually, their strange guest began asking them questions, trying to piece himself back together faster and faster.

"I was in a place with a high rock on one side."

"You were next to, what, a cliff? Maybe a mountain?"

"I was next to a mountain. We looked for bright and shining stone. I was good at finding it."

"JD, you dog, you're saying you were a prospector? Did you hit it big? Can I borrow a dollar?"

"I am a prospector. I hit it big. You can not borrow a dollar."

Eventually, of course, serious matters came up, as the captain considered potential legal ramifications. "JD, do you have any idea why they dumped you from that freighter?"

"The crew of the freighter found me in a shipping crate. They saw I was dead."

"They thought you were dead, you mean."

"They thought I was dead."

"JD, why were you in a shipping crate?"

"I was thought killed by men who wanted my gold."

"You got claim-jumped?"

"I got claim-jumped. They wanted my gold. They thought I was dead. What does a man do when that happens?"

The captain, now more alarmed than ever, consoled JD to speak to the law, to get legal representation.

Of course, the crew told JD what a real man would do.

The Imposter was ever-so-concerned with proper imitation.

* * *

The saloon's owner didn't want a risen Jimmy Dougherty in his establishment any longer than he had to be, and was more than happy to give Sallie the night off to get the formerly-deceased out of there. She walked with Jimmy, as he made a bee-line for the nearby general store. She tried to clean the sweat off his forehead with her handkerchief, but he softly caught her hands, and so she just held onto him as they walked, blushing.

"We all knew they did it, Jimmy, but the circuit judge said there wasn't any evidence that anything had happened to you. Said you might have just fallen into a crevice and...and died there."

"They thought I was dead. They put me in a shipping crate. The crew found me and thought I was dead and dumped me into the sea. Another ship found me. I have come back to do my business."

Sallie was quiet as they neared the old, creaking building that serviced the whole town's commercial needs. "You're acting strange, Jimmy, and I mean, after that I can't blame you, but...what are you going to do?"

"What a real man would."

"Jimmy...what does that even mean?" She stood aside as he neared the door, fearing what he'd do when he got there.

"Meet them with a gun in each hand."

Sallie tried not to cry as he moved to open the door, then blinked as he spoke again.

"Hands," Jimmy said helpfully, "are at the end of each arm," before disappearing inside.

* * *

Ed had the whole band creep towards town at the cusp of dawn. Mark Gravely had his big shotgun loaded for bear; Little Ed

Hendricks brought out his old military rifle and made sure all his powder was dry. Everyone else got out their revolvers, Ed breaking out his spares for anyone who was stupid enough to have lost theirs gambling.

"We messed this one up once. This time, we bury the bastard, people. I don't know about you, but I don't want to go back to being dirt-farmer poor again." They laughed, trying to keep their spirits up, and got ready to fill Jimmy full of lead, and not to think of what Ralph had said happened to dearly lamented Chuck.

* * *

The man called Jimmy Dougherty, called JD, called nothing, but who had twisted and turned himself into the form of this man, met them as they came into the town beneath the rosy fingers of the dawn. He stood there, grinning as they came, their guns raised, pointing at him from all sides as they skittered along the dusty edges of the town, trying to encircle him.

Ed Standing spat, eying up Jimmy from the rear of his pack of claim-jumpers.

"You're pretty stupid, kid. Should've run off when you had the chance. I can see you're sweating. Realized what a mistake you made, huh?" Nervous laughter followed from his bunch, everyone but Ralph working up to dismissive snickers of the foolish young man that stood before them.

Jimmy just smiled, and stretched, arms reaching outwards.

"You killed me and put me in a shipping box. I came back. Now I will deal with you like a real man."

Ed started to scream for everyone to shoot now, to put down the man in front of them, the thing that had come back from the dead, but his voice caught in his throat as he saw Jimmy pull a gun in every hand, in the forest of arms that seemed to erupt from the graceful figure, a gleaming arsenal of gun-after-gun-after-gun facing the claim-jumpers, eight gleaming barrels roaring.

All across the town, they could hear something like rolling thunder.

No one ever questioned Jimmy Dougherty** about how he dealt with Ed Standing's gang.

No one ever asked Jimmy Dougherty about why he was always sweating.

No one ever asked Jimmy Dougherty about why he and Sallie Anne Mayfield could never manage to have children.

No one ever dared, for Jimmy Dougherty was a real man.

This was just how the Imposter liked it.

Talk to Us

Danna Joy Staaf

Below his eyes, a dryped has two openings. One sticks out a little bit, and is like a siphon. He uses it to breathe.

And to defecate?

No. For that he has another opening, between his lower arms. Drypeds defecate in private, shut inside their dens, and do not talk about it.

Weird. The females do use their siphons to mate, though, right?

No, never. They have yet another opening for mating, also between the lower arms, but separate from the one for defecation. Mating is done in private as well, although they talk about it a little more.

Why do they need so many openings?

Let me finish, Speckled. I said there were two openings on the dryped's head. The second one, below his siphon, is a mouth.

What! Their mouth isn't hidden between their arms?

No, because they use it to talk.

They use their mouth to talk?

Yes.

That's really gross. Then do they also . . . eat . . . in public?

It is one of the most common things for drypeds to do. They are constantly going to one another's dens in order to eat together, and going out to special dens for the purpose of eating together.

Ugh. I'm glad they're leaving.

That is not a wise thing to be glad of.

* * *

Vella Pachik was eighty-three years old when she refused to evacuate Earth. If she played by the average human lifespan, she could expect another twenty years; with her genetics and lifestyle, it was more likely to be forty. She had a daughter on Mars and a son on the Moon, a grandson and a great-grandchild on Europa, and a granddaughter and two more great-grandchildren on Brahe. Her first husband had died in a Lunar mining accident that Vella had barely escaped. Her second husband's final research flight to Earth had gone down somewhere over the Pacific Ocean.

"Dr. Pachik," said the bureaucrat, in a tone of carefully mingled respect and authority. "You must be aware that the loss of the Calypso thirty years ago has been investigated by the SU in the most thorough manner. It is not possible that your husband is still alive."

"Why are you talking to me about my personal history?" inquired Vella, matching him for authority and dropping the respect. "We're discussing Legacy's plan to retain an Earth presence."

The bureaucrat fumbled. "I, ah, our psychologist has analyzed the profiles of your group, Dr. Pachik. The variety of probable individual motivations for wishing to defy Evacuation are quite, ah, understandable. But the people have spoken; SU favors full removal; exceptions cannot be made."

Vella leaned close, invading the man's personal space until she could count the drops of sweat on his upper lip. Sea levels were high, the ice caps long gone, and it was hot and humid in the Berlin coastal rocket base. Vella was glad that the land had been reclaimed by the ocean, that the talktopus were busily exploring the ruins of Los Angeles, Buenos Aires, and Venice. What she wasn't happy about was humanity's determination to cut contact and leave them to it.

"Our personal motivations are none of your business," she said. "Your business is to address Legacy's objections and proposal, as presented repeatedly to the SU, and just as often ignored."

She tapped on the wall of text beside them. These arguments had been posted and re-posted for years, ever since the SU began to debate Evacuation. But here, at Legacy's live-streamed last stand, she decided to say it all again. For clarity. And for drama.

"We, the members and supporters of Legacy, are in agreement with the official proclamation released by the Solar Union that *Dictopus sapiens*, commonly known as the talktopus, is fully sentient and conscious, with the same capabilities of language, tool use, artistic expression, and morality possessed by humans.

"However, Legacy finds the the subsequent assertion that *D. sapiens* 'merits the opportunity to grow and develop independent and free of outside influence' sadly lacking in scientific or historic understanding. Neither *Homo sapiens* nor any other species has ever developed free of outside influence, nor indeed would it be possible to do so. Legacy refuses to acquiesce to the totalitarian demand, based on this fallacious reasoning, that humans quit the planet Earth and leave it to the dominion of *D. sapiens.*"

It had been hard for Vella to understand how most humans—including her own children—could support Evacuation. Then again, most humans—including her own children—had never been to their planet of origin and didn't much care what happened to it. Surprisingly, it was the Extra-Solars (or, as they were commonly called, the Excess) who had dug in their heels. "We chose our exile from Earth," wrote Vella's granddaughter. "We know what it's like, and it shouldn't be forced on anyone. Certainly not on *everyone.*"

But Excess support for Legacy didn't translate into physical bodies on the ground. Only a handful of Legacy Solars, like Vella, were already on Earth, or could fly there in time to join the protest. So it was necessary to make as much of a fuss—a noble, peaceful fuss—as possible. Fortunately, the media were eating it up. Their aims were the same as Legacy's: a high-profile story and lots of views.

"The reasons for Legacy's position are threefold," Vella explained. "First, we reject the paternalistic assumption that humans know what is best for another sentient species. Second, we seek the understanding that may be gained from continuous contact with our only known fellow sentient in the universe. Third, we argue that SU cannot enforce Evacuation without violating its own charter, which makes explicit the human right to free movement, migration, and residence in habitable regions, barring only public health concerns—which are manifestly absent in this case."

Vella closed with a sweeping gesture around the planet, and turned back to the bureaucrat. Caught up in her own rhetoric, she almost expected him to be smiling and clapping.

Instead, his arms were folded, and he looked weary. "The last shuttle leaves in the morning, and it's my job to make sure every human on Earth is on that shuttle."

Vella narrowed her eyes and folded her own arms. Dusk fell as they played a game older than *Homo sapiens*: the staring contest.

* * *

Fivepapillae Speckled reached a casual arm around Manyfolds Bluespot as their cart rolled down the street. Bluespot gave him a dirty look. *That had better not be your hectocotylus, little boy.*

Of course not, answered Speckled, trying to appear shocked. *My fathers raised me right. I don't try to mate a matriarch until she asks.*

I'm not a matriarch yet, she flashed back. *And don't try to sound so experienced. You've never been asked.*

I've been waiting for you. Speckled hoped this would seem flattering, rather than pathetic.

Well, you can keep waiting. Bluespot slipped out from under his arm and moved to the front of the cart. *We're only on the most important mission in the history of the world. A little focus please?*

Fivepapillae Darkwave, one of Speckled's fathers, waved an arm to catch his attention. *When you're done trying to flirt, you might want to take a look outside.*

Speckled stretched his eyes above the water level to see what Darkwave and the others were looking at, but the cart rolled to a stop before he could find it. *Don't stop cranking, you idiot,* said Yellowline, one of the Fivepapillae family matriarchs.

Sorry! Speckled resumed turning the wheels of their cart, and tried to keep the embarrassment from showing on his skin. He'd only been brought along to power their transportation, because he was unusually large and strong for his age, and if he couldn't even do that, he wasn't likely to impress Bluespot, or Manyfolds Sevenarm, the elderly matriarch of Bluespot's family.

Not that he cared about impressing them, he reminded himself. Generations before Speckled was born, the Fivepapillae and Manyfolds had formed a small but fierce pro-dryped alliance. Speckled, however, had never seen a dryped and couldn't understand his family's fascination with them. At almost two years old, he was tired of being taught by Darkwave and his other fathers. He couldn't wait to strike out on his own and join a new family. A normal family.

A family with beautiful matriarchs who would welcome Speckled's strength and size, who would put him to work hunting crabs and building dens, and mate with him over the years as they aged into mothers. And when they laid their eggs and died, Speckled would be gracious to the other fathers and let them think that some of the hatchlings were theirs, and they would all raise the little ones together. Speckled would be a lot more fun than his own fathers, Darkwave and Redring and Stripes. Darkwave especially was so boring, always pushing Speckled to learn more and more of the stupid static colorless dryped language.

Yes, he would go to a good strong anti-dryped family. Maybe he would become Smoothback Speckled. Or Curledmiddlearms Speckled. But then, the Curledmiddlearms had eaten one of his hatchling sisters when she was just a few months out of the egg. And the Smoothbacks, he'd heard, were the reason Manyfolds Sevenarm had only seven arms. Certainly any family that chose to accept Speckled wouldn't eat him—or his arms. But if they chose *not* to accept him, they might tell him with their beaks, rather than their skin.

Speckled's eyes moved involuntarily to the Manyfolds. Of course it was no good joining a family that was just as dryped-crazy as his own. But Bluespot was really pretty. And she smelled good.

She noticed him looking, and turned around. *Did you see them?*

Speckled had forgotten they were all watching something. He poked his eyes back out of the water and stared into the dark.

Look, over there, said Bluespot. She pointed to an area, far in the distance, that was lit up more brightly than any bioluminescence Speckled had ever seen.

Are those drypeds? he asked. Creatures were moving in the light, now visible and then invisible between the huge structures that Darkwave had said were dryped dens. *They're so jerky. They don't bend right. How could they possibly have built all this?*

They know a lot more than we do, Speckled, Darkwave reminded him. *They made most of the materials we used to build this cart.*

Speckled waited until he was sure everyone was looking away, then sulked, *If they know so much, and they want to leave, maybe we should let them.*

* * *

"There are pockets of Legacy all over Earth," said Vella. She had hoped it wouldn't come to this. She had hoped to win by logic, not pragmatism, but she would win. "You can't root us all out without disrupting the planet, and therefore the talktopus, far more than we will do if we simply stay."

The bureaucrat rubbed his temples. He was getting a headache. The only people left on Earth were a handful of his fellow paper-pushers, a skeleton police force, a salivating media crew, and these damned Legacy people. "So what is this?" he said. "Some kind of civil disobedience?"

Vella spread her hands. "We don't believe we are disobeying. In fact, we believe that to retain a human presence on Earth is in the spirit of strict obedience to the first mandate of the SU."

"The first mandate explicitly excludes the occupation of and expansion into previously inhabited regions." He waved an arm. "Earth is inhabited, Dr. Pachik, and not by humans."

"But not *previously* inhabited. If we discovered a new world with a sentient species, of course we would avoid settlement and engage in only the most cautious and respectful contact, ready to terminate at any time at the ruling of the ethicists. But surely you can see that in the case of Earth, we're not taking over the talktopus' planet. If anything, they're taking over *our* planet."

"We were hardly using it," he reminded her.

"But we *were* here first, and we have, for better and worse, left our footprints for the talktopus to find—abandoned cities, nuclear waste, endless plastics. It is the grossest carelessness to pretend the human occupation of Earth never happened, to leave our technological leftovers to the talktopus without also sharing our knowledge."

The bureaucrat's eyes gleamed, and Vella wondered what she had given him to latch on to. He glanced around to make sure the media were still recording. As if they would stop. "You accuse the SU of paternalism, but isn't this even worse? You think you know what's best for the talktopus? Our culturalists predict they won't want us around. They certainly haven't begged us to stay, have they?"

"Well, why don't we go out and ask them?" Vella felt the sarcasm rising. She was too tired to fend it off. "Oh—we're not allowed to *ask* them what they want, because of Non-Interference."

"The talktopus are free to engage with humans, if they wish. They have not shown any inclination to do so."

"Because we live on land!" Vella was getting frustrated, which wouldn't look good. She tried to go back to earnest scientific detachment. "And because their entire concept of language is visual, not spoken. It's not possible for them to hear, much less understand, our language."

"They read, don't they?"

"A few hundred years ago, one scientist taught a handful of

talktopus to read. But as soon as the SU found out, the lab was shut down. For the talktopus, that was fifty generations ago. What are the odds that the knowledge has survived, much less spread?"

"I don't know, ma'am," the bureaucrat said. "But I know Non-Interference, and I know Evacuation. And if I can't root out all the members of Legacy, at least I'll start with you. Would you like to leave the planet conscious or unconscious?"

* * *

I'm hungry. Will you crank for a second?

Fine. Be quick. Bluespot grasped the crank and kept her eyes focused forward while Speckled slipped to the back of the cart and enveloped one of the snails stashed there as emergency snacks. It was rude to eat in such close quarters, but he'd been working hard. He slurped down the snail as fast as possible, then returned to Bluespot.

Thanks. I'll take it back now.

Did he imagine that she let their arms slide together as they traded positions? Probably he did. She didn't give him another look as she joined the matriarchs at the front of the cart.

No crabs, hard work, risk of death, he said to himself, following the rhythm of the crank. *When I come of age, I'm out of this pro-dryped crazy-den as fast as camouflage.*

He didn't think anyone was looking. But when Sevenarm drifted toward him, he realized she had seen his rant. She colored with surprising gentleness. *You are free to go wherever you wish once you leave your family, Speckled. But I hope that this glimpse of the drypeds will help you understand why we are willing to risk everything to convince them to stay.*

If we fail today, added Darkwave, *we lose their knowledge forever.*

Speckled wasn't sure that would be such a bad thing, but Bluespot looked alarmed. She glanced at her mentor. *What about those island drypeds you mentioned, Sevenarm?*

Sevenarm turned to the side and blew feces out of her siphon. At nine years old, she was starting to look frail, her body breaking down and turning itself into eggs. *One of my mother's mother's fathers came to the Manyfolds from far to the west, and claimed to have seen a few drypeds fall out of the sky onto island. I do not know the truth of it.*

Wouldn't they be dead by now anyway? asked Speckled.

Bluespot flickered in amusement. *Don't you even know, drypeds live for a hundred years.*

We used to say they were few and unchanging, the whales of dry land, said Sevenarm. *But now they are changing. Now they are leaving.*

Suddenly the carriage vibrated in a new way—not the bumps of the road or Speckled's careless cranking. Surprise and fear lit up everyone's skin. *The Smoothbacks must have followed us out of the water,* said Yellowline. *I can't see them. But they're within catapult range.*

The impact had cracked the cart. Speckled felt the water level dropping. *What do we do?*

Keep cranking, said Yellowline. *We must deliver our message to the drypeds.*

Are we going to die? asked Bluespot.

For a moment no one answered. *The drypeds have very fast carts,* said Darkwave finally. *They may be able to take us back to the ocean.*

Speckled cranked with all the power he could muster. After a few tense moments, the carriage shuddered with a second impact, then shattered.

Once or twice before, as a daredevil hatchling, Speckled had crawled out of the water onto land. Now that he was larger, he found it even more uncomfortable than he remembered. He was suddenly heavy and disoriented, squashed flat, struggling to breathe. He looked for the others.

There was Sevenarm, dragging herself over the ground, and Yellowline, oozing along beside her. *Crawl,* she commanded, when she saw Speckled. *Keep going toward the drypeds.*

But Speckled was too dazed to move. He saw that a piece of the broken cart had crushed Darkwave's head. The father's arms continued to stretch and curl of their own accord, though his skin flashed Death.

Another piece of the cart had torn Bluespot's mantle open. Her gills and stomach spilled out onto the ground, but her eyes met Speckled's. Her mantle was too damaged for her to speak clearly, but he understood a little from the patterns on her arms and head. *Go . . . time . . . water . . . go.*

Speckled crawled away and caught up with the matriarchs. He didn't want to think about whoever had attacked them and whether they might still be pursuing. Neither did he want to think about the disgusting drypeds in front of them.

He thought instead about his choice of a new family—if he lived to get back to the water. (*Not* living to get back to the water was another thing he didn't want to think about.) He'd planned for so long to go to an anti-dryped family. But he'd liked Bluespot, a lot. Her sisters were probably just as pretty. And he liked Sevenarm, too.

The night air was damp, but still their skin dried, from wet to sticky. Their muscles slowed and their vision blurred with lack of oxygen. *Yes,* thought Speckled inanely before he passed out, *as soon as we get back in the water I'll ask Sevenarm if I can join the Manyfolds.*

* * *

"Look, over by the water! Something just exploded!"

Vella looked up to see the distant wreckage. The media swarmed toward it, and the members of Legacy were quick to follow, with the bureaucrats and police trailing behind and mumbling about protocol. Vella was a spry eighty-three, but she was outpaced by the younger members of the group. As she hurried along, she pulled out a pair of glasses that would allow her to see the polarized channels in talktopus language. Several other members of Legacy and at least one of the media had also donned their glasses.

When Vella was still a little distance away, everyone in front of her stopped and hushed. "Is it dead?" she heard someone ask.

Vella put on a final burst of speed and reached the knot of humans. They let her push to the front, though the media bristled with questions. "What do you think happened here? Was it a suicide attempt? A runaway? A war?"

Vella didn't have any answers, so she gave them a mysterious shrug and a smile, then bent over the talktopus body. "Is it still alive?" they demanded.

"If certain scientific regulatory agencies had been a little less literal about Non-Interference," she told them, "I might have enough information to answer that." She pulled a water bottle from her hip, but was stopped by a desperate shout from the bureaucrat.

"Non-Interference!"

"Compassion toward all sentient beings," Vella shot back. The ancient words still had their power, and he subsided. Gently she dripped water onto the talktopus, then wet her own arms and lifted its body. Its arms dangled to her knees. "Let's see if we can do anything for you, big fella."

* * *

Speckled blinked several times. He was underwater. That was good. All his arms and senses seemed to be in working order. That was even better. He looked around, and saw that he was in a transparent container, surrounded by drypeds. That was not good at all.

The container was completely empty. There was nothing to sit on or fidget with or hide in. He stared through the walls at the drypeds. They were so—meaningless. Their colors and patterns didn't change at all.

Then he noticed that one of his walls did not look out at the drypeds, but instead showed him a very detailed high-contrast pattern. He moved closer, and recognized the dryped language that Darkwave had made him learn. Speckled had not been the best student. It took him a long time to piece the meanings together.

We will not hurt you. We will take you back to the water if you want.

Well, that's good news, Speckled said to himself. He kept reading.

We are sorry for the deaths of your companions.

He assumed they meant Darkwave and Bluespot, and he began to wonder where Yellowline and Sevenarm were. Could they be watching from other containers? He began calling out to them.

The ones you are calling for are dead, too. We are so sorry.

Whoa. Speckled went white with surprise. Tentatively, he patterned, *You can understand me?*

He looked out of a clear wall and saw the drypeds frantically moving their arms, as well as the little arms at the ends of their arms. Their mouths moved too, although he felt crass for noticing, and he supposed they were speaking to each other. They looked excited. He turned his gaze back to the patterned wall.

Yes, some of us can understand your language. But we weren't sure you could understand ours. This is wonderful! How did you—

After Speckled had laboriously translated that far, the patterns stopped. He looked out to see two drypeds making sharp gestures at each other. Suddenly he felt very tired. *They must have known.* Yellowline, Sevenarm, probably Darkwave, and maybe even Bluespot, must all have known that drypeds could understand their language, and that's why they were coming here. It was only he, the child, the idiot, the cranker, who didn't know.

And now they were dead. The Fivepapillae had only two teachers left, and one matriarch. As for the Manyfolds—the female he'd hoped to mate with was gone. The mother whose eggs would have renewed the family was gone. Maybe he should take a very long journey, like some young males did. Travel far away. Maybe the drypeds would take him to a different part of the ocean, if he asked.

His thoughts were interrupted by more high-contrast patterns on the wall.

Were you coming to see us for a reason?

Yes, he answered. *At least, they were. I was just the cranker.* That was the silliest part. He wasn't clever or knowledgeable or motivated. The only reason for his presence on the cart had been his strength. And in the end, it was that raw strength that had kept him alive when the others suffocated and dried out, killed by their devotion to *the most important mission in the history of the world.*

The drypeds asked, *Will you tell us?*

Speckled shut his eyes and crammed himself into one corner. He could pretend he didn't know the reason. He was only the cranker, after all. That would be the easiest way out. Or he could tell them anything he wanted. He was all that was left of the expedition. Another one would not be sent. Their families had no lives to spare. He could tell the drypeds anything—he could tell them he wanted them all to go away.

He opened his eyes and looked out again. The drypeds seemed agitated by his little retreat. It looked like someone was carrying a crab, and someone else was holding a round colorful object, and a third dryped was preventing either of those from approaching Speckled.

Hey hey, he flashed, *Crab yes. Crazy ball no.*

The ones holding things must not have been able to understand him, because they didn't move, but the third one took the crab and tossed it into the water. *Good job*, he told them, and ate it. He didn't care if they wanted to watch. It wasn't any of his business.

Then he looked back at the patterned wall. It still held the question: *Will you tell us?*

Speckled thought about the texture of Bluespot's skin when her arms rubbed against his. He thought about everything Darkwave had said they could learn from the drypeds. He wondered if he could use their fast carts to get revenge on the Smoothbacks who had killed his family. *Both* of his families, because he was sure he would join the Manyfolds now. If they let him.

And if he kept the drypeds from leaving, of course the Manyfolds would welcome him. He'd be a hero.

Will you tell us?

Yes. We want you to stay.

Empathy Evolving as a Quantum of Eight-Dimensional Perception

Claude Lalumière

1. Empathy

The human male is dying, his body incorrectly configured. Humans have long been extinct, but the biologist recognizes its primate physiology. She knows the creature should be externally symmetrical; that its head should be attached by a neck sprouting from the cavity at the top of the thorax; that its skeleton should be entirely internal; that its reproductive organs should dangle from its pelvis; that its four limbs should not be attached and joined together to its spine; that it should not be excreting so much fluid.

The biologist slides one arm over the primate oddity. Her suction cups try to gather information about the mammal; the human's pain is so absolute that it permeates his entire consciousness, interfering with data collection. The progenetic solution of the life-support shell has slowed the dying process but does not significantly lessen the creature's suffering. The biologist adjusts the composition of the serum, pumping more painkiller into the shell.

Three of the biologist's eight arms are massaging the human, tending to the animal. The fluid excreted by the deformed human seeps into the permeable flesh of the octopus biologist.

As her mind reaches out to his, his mind reaches out to hers. None of her subjects have ever reciprocated before; she has no armour with which to defend herself. When the human's relief from pain comes, it is sudden; it hits the octopus like a flash flood, and data streams—quantic and disorienting—whirlpool into her mind. The memories and experiences and perceptions and emotions of the two beings mingle and merge. The two individuals are utterly alien to each other—the octopus biologist and the human anomaly—yet they each become inexorably enmeshed with the other. For a span that lasts a plancktime in four-dimensional spacetime but for intermittent, syncopated perpetuity in eight-dimensional spacetime, they are mutually overcome by unexpected empathy and tenderness.

2. Evolving

The human comes from a time he calls "the 21st century"; in that era, there are large continents of land mass above sea level, and humans are the dominant species on the planet. Octopuses are food for the humans. Though this human chose not eat octopus, or any animal flesh at all. The biologist finds this odd. It excites her scientific curiosity, as does everything about this anomalous beast. The consumption of live flesh is the greatest ecstasy; oh, that delicious moment when the consciousness of the prey is subsumed to the will of the predator. She wonders about the taste of the human's flesh.

The human's data stream confirms a few of the biologist's ideas about the human era, but for the most part it is more alien than she had previously believed. She has eaten some mammals before, but the life-information she gleaned from these other animals did not prepare her for the reality of human history or how radically different the natural world was in this animal's time.

This, the octopus gleans before she and the human are quantically subsumed into each other.

3. As

There was an explosion; it killed two nearby octopuses. This animal was found among the rubble, then the biologist was brought to the site to study the strange beast. Normally, the meat would have been eaten by the three octopuses who found it. By law, this body belonged to them. But a consensus was reached by the trio. Could other explosions occur? Where they in danger? The strange animal should be examined as it was found before it could be consumed.

The biologist did not want to risk moving the fragile mammal. She brought her equipment to the site, handling the creature with utmost care. The anomalous mammal oozed a gooey fluid.

4. A

Professor Dexter Van yearns for escape, for a future where the Earth has rid itself of humanity. He feels no affinity for either his species or his time. Humanity's disregard for its own planet and for the others with whom it shares that planet disgusts him so profoundly that it has completely alienated him from his culture and species. His own unwilling complicity in the destruction of his homeworld and in the casual torture and thoughtless annihilation of countless nonhuman animals by human hand fills him with such self-loathing that he can barely sleep without the help of heavy medication.

The one thing that gives the professor any pleasure whatsoever is his absolute conviction that humanity is heading toward extinction, through a combination of blind self-destruction by the species itself and of the planet's self-regulating homeostatic system.

He wants to experience the posthuman future beyond the coming extinction event. To him, that world-to-be is home. Heaven on Earth.

And now he will get there. Away from the humanity he loathes more with each passing day of its miserable, despicable existence.

The time anchor will ensure that no matter how far in time he travels he will remain in the same relative space, compensating for Earth's orbit around Sol, the Solar System's circulation within the Milky Way, and the Milky Way's movement within the universe.

But time, he knows, is mostly a matter of perception. According to his calculations, he has perfected the correct cocktail of psychotropic drugs to propel his consciousness, and thus his physical self, into the far future. At least one hundred thousand years into the future. Perhaps as much as ten million years. But without experimentation he cannot be certain. Nevertheless, he does not hesitate.

He activates the time anchor, steps into it, and injects the psychotropic cocktail into his bloodstream.

5. Quantum

Professor Van's consciousness has escaped linear time; his body tried to reconfigure itself in the image of his new quantic perceptions and is now secreting a molecularly enhanced time-travelling cocktail. The octopus biologist's skin is permeable to the secretion. The octopus and the human are thus quantically subsumed into each other.

The lifespan of Dexter Van is re-experienced by the octopus biologist. In this revised timeline, that life follows a different path, guided from birth onward by octopus sentience.

This Dexter Van does not become an introverted vegan. Instead, he/she revels in being an omnisexual predator, an insatiable carnivore, and a brash alpha male. He/she is, however, as misanthropic as the original Dexter Van.

Few like, much less love, this Dexter Van, but his/her predatory alien personality proves to be addictive and alluring to those humans vulnerable to dominant wills.

This iteration of Dexter Van yearns for escape, for a future where the Earth has rid itself of this snivelling species, humans. The air of their world is foul, disgusting—a situation entirely of their own making. Their world is much too dry for his/her comfort. The civilization the humans have built is hard, sharp, vulgar, alienating. Their art is ugly and loud. He/she wants to return to the posthuman, octupus future—wants to return home. And he/she will get there.

At the same spacetime coordinates as the original Dexter

perfected time travel, the quantic human/octopus hybrid makes the same breakthrough.

The new Dexter Van activates the time anchor, steps into it, and injects the psychotropic cocktail into his/her bloodstream.

In the far future, there is an explosion; it kills two nearby octopuses. This animal is found among the rubble, then the biologist is brought to the site to study it.

The biologist is a female octopus animated since birth by the sentience of the human Dexter Van. The human consciousness of Dexter Van has barely been able to cope with octopus biology and cognition. The instant the human and the octopus had first interfaced, Van had experienced the entirety of the biologist's lifespan to that moment. Thus, he/she followed the map of the octopus's life as best he/she could, taking unexpected pleasure in the consumption of live animal flesh, experiencing unexpected and ecstatic empathy whenever his/her evolved octopus physiology subsumed the lives of prey.

Now he/she encounters his/her quantically reconfigured human body, which he/she never dared hope he/she would see again.

With better knowledge and experience, the Dexter Van octopus believes he/she can control the quantic time displacement and restore each consciousness to the correct body. He/she runs his/her octopus arms over the dying human body, absorbing the enhanced psychotropic cocktail it secretes.

6. Of

In the most likely timeline quantically fractalling from the moment when the hybridized versions of Dexter Van and the octopus biologist commune, the Dexter Van octopus succeeds in controlling the quantic time event created by the interface of the psychotropic cocktail with his displaced human consciousness. Multiple past timelines converge and merge into one octopus future, the one to which the restored Professor Dexter Van now travels safely, his body retaining its viable primate configuration. His point of arrival is the same, but this time he can shift the explosion caused by his arrival to a barren coordinate in quantic spacetime, thus killing no-one. The octopus biologist, now gifted with enhanced quantic time perception, knows to expect his arrival, and she is already there to welcome him.

She adopts him, and he becomes her beloved pet. At first, they understand each other perfectly, as their consciousnesses still connect at eight-dimensional nexus points. But gradually their minds resettle into linear four-dimensional timespace and their empathic connection abates gradually until, one year later, it disappears entirely. They become like strangers. Still, there remain vestiges of mutual understanding.

A month after their connection is entirely severed, the octopus biologist is killed in one of the many duels she has had to fight to maintain her claim on Dexter Van. The human—the only such creature in this era—is much coveted among the octopus population.

The human escapes before his new octopus owner can lay claim to him, but without protection Van is, within hours, assaulted and devoured by an orcalion, the deadliest wild predator in this posthuman future.

7. Eight-Dimensional

In eight-dimensional spacetime, Dexter Van and the octopus biologist merge into one humanoid/cephalopod creature that exists simultaneously at the edge of probability at quantic fractal coordinates across various timelines. The quantic hybrid is only vaguely perceivable by those whose consciousness is in some way untethered from the linear causality of four-dimensional spacetime. Visionaries, artists, prophets, mystics, and junkies are among those few able to partially perceive the quantic hybrid.

God. Demon. Hallucination. Nightmare. Hero. Villain. Object of worship. Omen of doom.

Perpetually alone and alienated from any reality, the hybrid creature struggles to communicate with those few who can almost perceive it.

But the meaning and intent of its attempts at communication is quantically garbled by being translated from eight dimensions into four dimensions, turning its speech into vaguely menacing gibberish: *bsh'rob-nakada dakegag-rua'll rnau-at'tha g'ghokhugga-shlagak g'tomo-p'cthu g'bakothl-shiggoth zathub-gthul'uh yuat-uach-k'thon...*

8. Perception

Time stops. From Professor Dexter Van's perspective. The moment of arrival. One infinitesimal plancktime lasting a subjective infinity. Dexter Van. The only extant human. Evolved octopuses. Immobile as statues.

Outside. The world. A still life. The octopus future. Moss. Mould. A bed of water covers the ground. Thick damp air.

Van roams the world. The watery Earth. Advanced greenhouse conditions. Scant but surprising evidence of human ruins. Strange new flora. Strange new fauna. Giant ambulatory cephalopods. Quadruped fish.

Frogs. Toads. Lizards. Birds. Weird new iterations. Occupying different biological niches from their ancestors. Predatory plants devour small amphibious mammals. Halted mid-action.

Everything. Unmoving. Alive. Weird and wondrous. Rot. Renewal. Health. Evolution.

A global portrait of planetary survival. Lasting one infinitesimal infinite plancktime. Dexter Van's eternal afterlife. Heaven. Nirvana. A new Eden. Earth. Blissfully rid of humanity.

Octopus. Dominant. Ubiquitous art. Elaborate stone gardens. Sculptures. Resplendent colours. Everywhere. Beauty.

Each plancktime is an infinite quantic spacetime coordinate. Van does not exist in the next plancktime. Beyond the range of Dexter Van's quantic perception. Time moves forward, unaffected by the quantic anomaly. Equation: $1 = 8 = \infty = 0$. The octopus biologist never encounters Professor Dexter Van. The dreams of her multiversal alter egos converge. Octopus dreams of xenophilic empathy in quantic fractals.

Unearthly Pearl

Brenda Anderson

I dip my fingers in the votive bowl. The pearl dust feels like silk. When it is ground, sifted and strained, my workers pour its silky powder into large, shallow votive bowls, so that it is easier to throw in the air. Brides want the blessing of the sea, and it falls on them as they drift towards their grooms. The air clouds, becomes milky, fecund. Poets tell us much about the consummation of love. Pearls say it all.

I dip my fingertips once more. The powder feels so natural against the skin, so warm. Of course brides choose pearl. I would, too.

I send my divers to find and collect the pearls themselves, which I grade before they're ground and packaged. I match colours every day until late at night. There is a world of difference between blush pink and damask rose. Brides know.

The door opens and I turn my wheelchair. Telf walks towards me, left hand behind his back. We exchange pleasantries, employer to business partner. "Working late again, Mina? You work too hard, too many hours, too much eyestrain. It's not good for your health. Of course it's all been worth it."

He isn't here to discuss my health. What does he hold behind his back? For some reason I feel nervous.

"I have a gift for you, Mina. With this, you can retire," he says.

I am a wealthy woman, I could retire anytime. In all his years working for me, Telf has never been one to waste words. He is hardworking, ambitious. This must be important to him.

"Imagine being able to dive again," he says and smiles. I flinch. Since my accident I've been paralysed from the waist down, and haven't returned to the water. Diving was my passion and my source of income. I know the best places to find pearl. I dived them all.

"Meet Fred," says Telf. He presents me with a large box. Inside, I see a dark shape. Suddenly, a long black tentacle shoots forward and wraps around my shoulders. I cry out, startled. Telf smiles and holds a finger to his lips.

"Careful. Don't frighten him," he says.

"Him?" I pull back. Its sucker pads quiver, as if the creature finds something surprising.

"It," concedes Telf. "Though it's hard to tell the difference. This type of cephalopod is native to half a dozen water planets and has a knack for finding pearl. Fred will be the perfect diving harness for you." I draw in my breath. I am embarrassed by my twisted body. Before, I had the grace and limbs of a dancer. It has been so long since I dared to dream of diving. "What do you say, Mina?"

"Get it off me," I gasp.

The black tentacle immediately withdraws, with no intervention from Telf. So. Fred understands speech? How amazing. I swallow.

"With Fred's arms as your harness, you could re-enter the world of pearls," says Telf. "This is a wonderful opportunity for you, Mina."

In my mind I see a beautiful gold-hued pearl in the shape of a teardrop, a freak of nature worth a fortune. Where is this pearl? Why do I see it so clearly? I shake my head. "An octopus, Telf? No offence to our alien friend here, but I'd rather use my own body."

< would you? > A silky voice, inside my head. I start.

"Did you say something?" I ask. Telf looks puzzled at my question, and shakes his head. He looks impatient.

"It's very cooperative, Mina. Why not start soon? You two can use the training tank to get accustomed to one another."

< don't listen to him > pleads the voice. < he's anxious to get you in the tank, because he's tampered with its filters. when you lose consciousness he will blame the accident on me >

I keep my face tranquil. Telf is ambitious, but why should I trust an alien cephalopod?

"How did you find this creature, Telf?"

Telf laughs, but I hear a false note. "A happy accident. In a large vat that cleared customs, but not quarantine. It probably spent years getting to this size. An investment, for our business."

I shake my head. "Telf, my time is spent grading and sorting the pearls. No cephalopod can do that."

< wrong > says Fred, and in his silky voice I hear truth. < pearls are the mainspring of our society. blindfolded, I can grade pearls by any criteria you like. we have sensitivities you humans can only dream about. I wish I could show you >

I wish it too. Who would I rather believe? In my mind's eye, I see myself harnessed to this pearl expert, wrapped in comfort while

its other arms propel us into new crevices and spaces unimaginable to humans. My breathing device winds through cephalopod and human extremities. Together we make a formidable team. Now I am the impatient one.

I tell Telf to leave the octopus with me, and I bid him goodnight. He leaves reluctantly. When he's gone, the cephalopod expresses relief. Alone together, he opens to me and describes his home world, how he grew to his present size during a long interstellar flight, how his race grows pearls within their bodies. I exchange information about our bivalves. He reacts to the notion that oysters can be farmed for pearls. In his society, the first pearl grown within the cephalopod's body is the most prized, the most beautiful. The notion of the 'first pearl' becomes too emotional for him to continue, so I let him rest.

The following day an inspection of the diving tank reveals tampering, exactly as Fred warned. I immediately fire Telf, upgrade my security and spend the next day with my lawyers.

Not long afterwards, Fred and I make our first dive together. I have no words for this happiness. Though Fred is neither husband, male, nor even human, we are one. I quickly learn to send my thoughts, and receive his. He explains that his race connects emotions with pearls, and asks for my understanding. The following day Fred gives me the gold teardrop pearl I saw in my mind's eye. I touch it with my fingertip, in awe at its size, shape and colour. This is it. His first pearl.

I have found a soul mate from the sea. I keep the gold pearl in a belt round my waist, like his arms. I am a bride indeed.

Daughters of Tethys

Camille Alexa

At the Temple gong's second chime I struggle my gown strap over my shoulder and slip my hand into Ianthe's rocky pool. The water is cooler than the air, though my ceph companion thrives in the moist warmth of the Temple caverns. Seeing my hand, she shoots eagerly from her favorite resting spot, an enormous empty nautilus shell gathered by one of my predecessors down by the shore.

On reaching me, she slows. Her violet arms curl up in excited greeting, then unfurl gently across my skin. Smiling, I dip even lower into the pool, water past my elbow, lapping at my shoulder, soaking the fabric of the gown which will quickly become sodden anyway in the warm eternal mists of the Temple outside our grotto.

"Good morning Ianthe, my lilac beauty," I say. Her color pulses even deeper as she wraps her suckers around my arm, winds onto my limb and hauls herself up out of the pool. She settles about my throat like a heavy, off-kilter necklace, four arms clasping around my neck, one trailing across my shoulder, two anchored lightly to my chest and the last, as is her habit, winding up through my damp hair to rest on the smooth spot behind my ear.

Withdrawing my hand, I glance at the glittery reflective surface of the pool, ripples in the clear water making us appear to shimmer in the moist air. The constant drip at the back of our grotto where it feeds Ianthe's pool is as familiar to me as my own heartbeat, as familiar as the feel of my ceph companion's suckers gliding over my skin or the keen look in her golden eyes.

Together we stand, each of us subtly, unconsciously, shifting weight and balance and grip to accommodate the other. I slip into my sandals, push aside the heavy beaded curtain, and try not to look as if I hurry too much down the passage while the gong rings its eighth and final chime, calling the three thousand Daughters of Tethys to the main Temple cavern to greet the Sons.

* * *

Most of the Daughters are already gathered in the large cave, their ceph companions bright jewels adorning the women's throats, wrists, shoulders. Many backs and cheeks and arms show the delicate tattooing left by light sucker venom, swirls and circles patterning skin in elaborate designs unique to each woman's ceph. Wenn sees us, smiles, comes to join Ianthe and me where we stand at the base of the goddess statue cupping the eight planets in her eight powerful arms. I scoop a palmful of water from the statue's pool, drizzle it over Ianthe, offer my open palm to Wenn so she can wet a finger.

"You get a good night's sleep, Saff?" she asks me, letting the moisture drip from her fingertip onto her tiny azure ceph. "I did. Figured with the Sons arriving, I was going to need it."

"Don't be vulgar, Wenn," I say. She laughs. Her companion Acaste is a fullgrown octopod the size of a large pearl. The little ceph pulses a brilliant blue where she clasps the base of Wenn's finger, a living sapphire ring.

Ianthe shifts one of her arms where it clasps two others at the back of my neck, the weight of her body resettling along my shoulder, solid and comforting. Here in the Temple, water hangs heavy in the air, visible droplets of mist soaking my gown, my hair, making the covered lanterns sparkle through my eyelashes where moisture beads. My Sisters and their octopod companions glide through the room with the usual languid grace for which we are known. Only I am awkward and ungraceful: too tall, too late, always scurrying through Temple passageways to meet the last chime. I often wonder why I was chosen that day from all the girls of my village, when the retiring Daughter and her beautiful companion, a mimic octo who changed the colors of her limbs with each passing moment, brought Metis. Every girl of the proper age gathered at the sea's edge, waited in water up to her knees with her skirts tucked into her belt while Metis, a plain coral octo the size of my fist with long curling limbs, meandered first around the ankles of one girl, then another, tasting our skin with her delicate cups until she found me, and didn't let go. The Daughter of Tethys brought me to take her place, live in her grotto at the Temple. That was the day I left my father and three sisters in the small fishing village, and came to join the three thousand Sisters here.

Metis is gone of course, her hundred thousand babies released into the Ocean. All but one; all but my lovely Ianthe, the daughter of my first ceph companion, who chose to remain with me and become my next.

Sorrow over Metis's passing rises in my throat, but I swallow it down. The rhythms of the Ocean and the rhythms of our lives are as they are, woman and octopod, tide and current, life and birth and death all lapping at the shores of the world with varying degrees of gentleness and force.

A flurry of activity at the other end of the Temple hall announces the arrival of the Sons, our brother order from the other side of the island. They've been traveling for days, making their yearly warm slow journey around the coast to us.

Ianthe shudders against the side of my throat where she clings, as though tasting my thoughts through my skin where her sensitive suckers adhere. Will she be receptive this year? Sometimes the cephs aren't. Sometimes they don't respond to the male octos, leaving their human companions to drink and dance and mingle all night long, but retire at last to their grottoes alone.

Well, not alone—we always have each other, we Daughters of Tethys: octopod and woman, woman and octo. It's the men who are visitors. The men and their cephs.

Unlike us, the Sons of Tethys carry their octos in open pouches slung low across their fronts. The waterproof slings bulge with seawater, swaying slightly with each man's gait as he files into the enormous chamber. Though our temples are small cities, each maintaining a population of precisely three thousand to honor the three thousand Sons and the three thousand Daughters of Tethys and Oceanus, not all bond with a companion. Some of the dry Sisters, who live outside the grottoes in light and air, weave among us now, carrying wood platters heaped high with sundried sea plums dipped in wild honey, or figs and dates traded for our intricate shellwork with villages down the coast. Other dry Sisters carry beaten silver trays covered in glass tumblers full of the smoky amber wine we make here, harvesting briny grapes from the tangled vines covering seaside cliffs.

I accept a glass gratefully from a passing tray, smiling quick and light at the Sister holding it steady for me. Wenn takes two glasses, downs one quickly and waves the girl on. "They never look comfortable inside the Temple caves, do they?" she asks, leaning close but not keeping her voice particularly low. "They always look . . . bedraggled."

Anyone would see what she means. Wenn herself is beautiful in the light mist of the caves. Her hair curls neatly about her ears in tight black crescents. Her sodden gown clings to her curves. Her tiny, brightly cyanophoric octo glows blue on her finger, enhancing and enhanced by Wenn's lean tapered hand.

The dry Sister moving away from us pauses, wipes water from her eyes awkwardly with one forearm, trying to keep the balance of her tray. The gown clumping at her thighs bunches inelegantly when she moves forward again, her feet slap wetly in her sandals.

"Not everyone is suited to the grottoes," I say, remembering my first weeks in the caves, the dark warmth of the moist passageways and the constant echoes of the dripping. I had lovely Metis with me always, of course. My hours were filled with my endless fascination for her ways: watching her dart after prey underwater, watching her swim, watching her walk with her mysterious sliding grace from one pool to the next in the communal feeding gardens.

"Not everyone," agrees Wenn. "But that one certainly is."

The arriving men have begun to mingle. It always amazes me how confident they seem, how unfettered the motions of masculine walking, how their arms swing and their legs stride. The man Wenn is admiring nearby laughs at something our Sister Rell murmurs at him in her coquettish way. Rell's octo, Calypso, is a lovely xanthophore, large and heavy-limbed, draped over her human companion's head with all eight arms curling gracefully down Rell's back like damp tresses of vibrant yellow, shiny and bright. Rell leans close, giving the octopod in the man's water-sling a chance to reach out, to taste her if it wants. But the man looks up, sees me looking. We recognize each other in an instant.

"He's headed this way!" squeaks Wenn. I forget she's even younger than I. She's one of the rare Sisters actually born here in the Temple, and as such always seems to know more than the rest of us, initiated to the Ocean's mysteries from an early age.

With a distracted wave to Rell and a cursory nod of greeting directed at Wenn, the man stops in front of me, lifts my hand, holds it between his like a clam between its shells.

"Saff," he says to me, sending a deep shiver from the base of my spine all the way up into Ianthe at my throat. She shivers in echo, and wraps an arm around my ear. I imagine her studying him with her golden gaze. I see his new ceph's iridophoric eyes glinting at me from his satchel sling. A coral reef octopod, like mine.

"Lonn." I say his name, not pretending to misremember—how could I? He smiles. I barely notice Wenn being led away by a short attractive man with a tiny ceph in a sling dangling at his neck, more a necklace pouch than a satchel. Lonn is watching Ianthe slide from one side of my throat to the other, her limbs trailing across my damp breasts. The glass globe lanterns make his wet skin look shiny, as though cast in bronze.

He gestures at Ianthe. "Is this from Metis?"

I nod, absently holding a finger for Ianthe to grasp with one elongated arm, wrap around several times. "Ianthe, born after last year. From Metis and Strymon."

At mention of his old ceph companion, I see the same sadness briefly light his eyes which burdens my heart when I think of Metis. For an instant, I wonder how I will bear year after year after year of losing companions, of nurturing them, living with them, loving them, and watching them die with a regularity governed by tides, by seasons, by the rhythm of the Ocean and of life itself. I have a sudden urge to turn and run from the Temple, taking Ianthe with me, leaving all the men and their octos and the unwavering, overwhelming will of the Ocean behind.

But then the selfishness of such a thing hits me and shame floods in, rushes back to fill my empty spaces with humility and regret, like saltwater rushing to fill shallow rocky pools with the tide.

"I'm sorry," I say. He doesn't answer, perhaps taking my words as sympathy for his dead companion. At least we Daughters are given a chance to bond with our octos' offspring. The men have to wait in

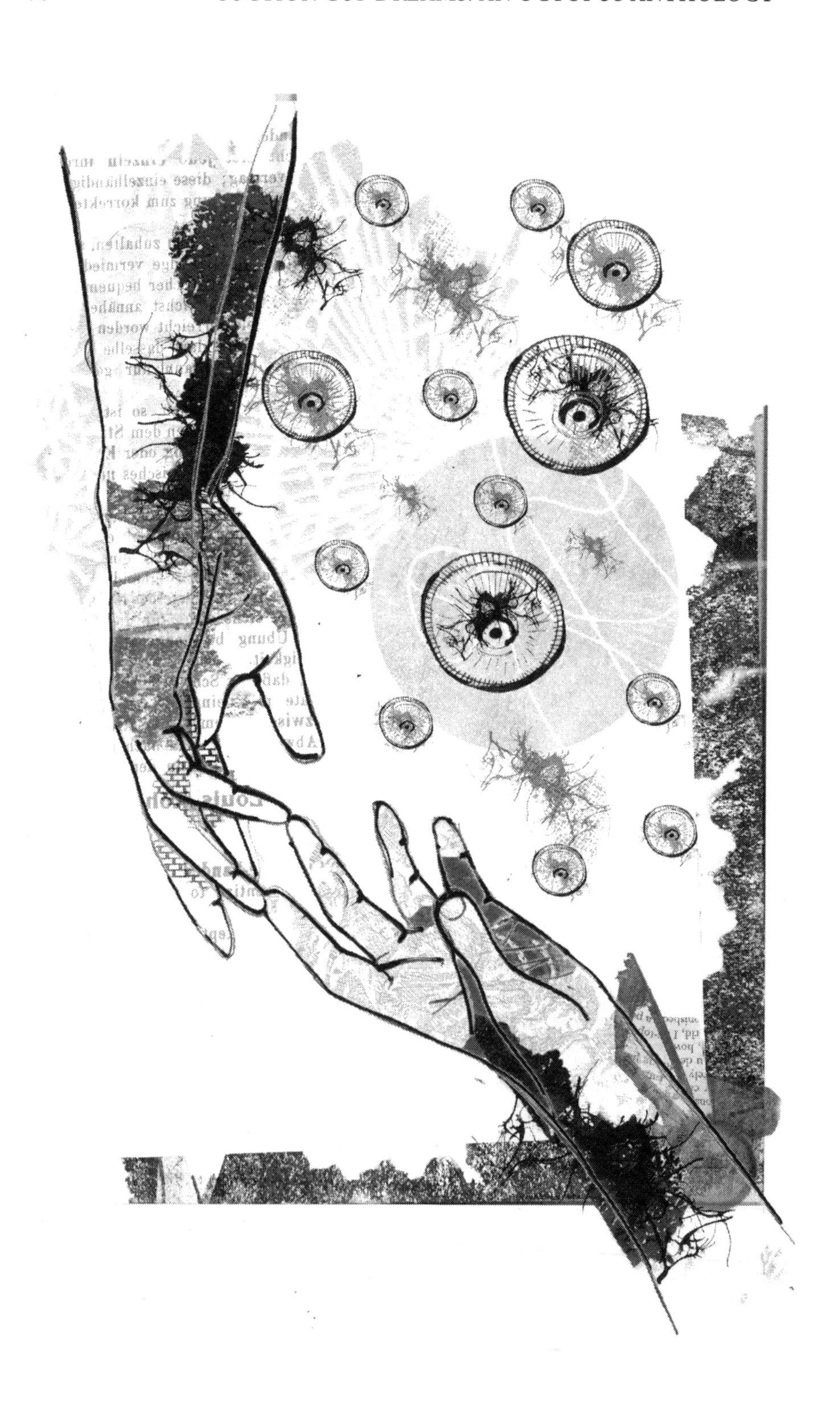

salt lagoons and shallow coves, letting wild cephs come taste their naked limbs, waiting for Tethys to guide one to accept him as its companion, to travel with him to this foreign shore and mate with another of Tethys's chosen.

The Temple cavern has grown loud with laughter and talk and simmering purpose. The dry Sisters—wet tonight, of course, and as Wenn noted, bedraggled—have circulated with too many trays of amber wine to count. Here and there, couples already begin to press close to one another, their cephs questing forth to entangle arms, or the male octopods venturing from their satchels, turning their limbs upside down and outward to display rows of enlarged suckers. My Sisters laugh and flirt, the men with them laugh and respond, and the briny scent of sex hangs as heavy in the air as the droplets of water gathered on my lashes, or running down the front of my gown between my breasts.

A tickle so light I don't first notice it among the trickling drops grows bolder. Glancing down, I see Lonn's octo, whose name I don't even know, has pulled itself up out of the waterfilled satchel. With four arms it balances on the open rim of the sling, two more limbs anchored solidly in the water, another touching Lonn's chest lightly—more for comfort than for balance, I decide. The eighth arm has crossed the short gulf between us, and is painting little patterns in the moisture on my skin. Ianthe pulses against my throat in a rhythm I've never felt from her before. It's silly, I know, but I can't help holding my breath as she reaches for the male ceph's arm, twines it with hers.

I glance up into Lonn's face, knowing he'll be watching me, not them. He is. It's neither encouraged nor discouraged to partner with the same man as the year before. It's the cephs who make the choice. Our octopods, our companions, our joy and burden and our sacred honor.

He reaches for my hand, laces his fingers with mine the way our octopods lace their limbs. Stepping close, moving together and slowly so the cephs can maintain their link, we make our way from the cavern. We aren't the only ones; couples are leaving, two by two, or rather, four by four. Silently, I lead Lonn through the rocky passages to my grotto chamber, the knowledge of what comes next licking across my ribs, up my spine, down my thighs. Ianthe tastes the excitement in me through my skin, my heartbeat, the quickening of my pulse. She trembles.

Reaching for the beaded curtain to our grotto and its clear clean pool, I try not to think of the beautiful garlands of eggs Ianthe will soon string in those shallow waters, decorating the pocked rock with lacy strands of future octos strung like tiny pearls. She will soon lose all interest in me, and spend the next month wafting warm currents across her hundred thousand eggs, and nourishing them, and protecting them from the predators I would never let come near her. And when she's done, and her hundred thousand babies glitter in our grotto's lanternlight, like stars reflected in the Ocean, she will die, having starved herself so they might live. As her companion, it will be my sacred duty to make sure her babies thrive, and grow, and are eventually carried to the shore and released into the cruel, glorious, boundless waters of Tethys, where they'll be free to live and mate and die on their own terms. If I'm lucky, one of them—just one out of the hundred thousand—will be moved by Tethys to stay, to cling to me as her brothers and sisters swim free, to honor me with her companionship and her beauty.

But that's all tomorrow, and tomorrow, and tomorrow. Tonight is tonight, and Lonn's hand is warm in mine as I lead him to the pool, his ceph's suckers lying lightly across my shoulder where the octo has ventured from his sling. Ianthe is a familiar weight at the base of my throat, her arms a familiar tug at the back of my neck. The water is warm as I lower myself into the briny pool, my gown billowing out, baring my naked limbs beneath, Lonn's eyes sweet and almost sad as they glint in the lantern's glow.

The Octopus Garden

D. Thomas Minton

Pieces of sky lay scattered in the rust-red mud. A warm breeze rippled the cotton-puff clouds until the reflections were gone, leaving only puddles. Tomoa, hands in pockets, suit coat flapping in the ocean breeze, stared at a solitary survey flag in the expanse of mud.

"You don't believe me?" said Pa'ali. The construction foreman looked from Mitchell to Tomoa, as if expecting his fellow Pacific Islander to come to his assistance.

Tomoa pushed at a ridge in the mud with the toe of his Italian leather shoe. Dozens of furrows sliced across the empty construction site to the ocean's edge. "You must admit," he said, "your story is hard to believe."

"I tell you, the waters rose, like great arms, and swept it all out to sea." Pa'ali's face glistened in the afternoon heat. "Why would I lie?"

"No tsunami was recorded by the DART2 buoy array." Mitchell stood next to their idling SUV, mopping sweat from his neck with a monogrammed handkerchief.

Tomoa admired the older man's ability to cut to the facts, but that was part of Mitchell's reputation. Mitchell had spent the entire twenty-six hours of their trip from Landtel headquarters in Seattle reviewing gigabytes of information on the Vatua resort project so he could efficiently isolate the truth from the chaff. He was Landtel

Corporation's "fix-it" man, which was good for the company, but bad for Tomoa.

"I'm not—"

"We've seen enough," Tomoa said. He removed his smart phone. He needed to re-establish himself as the man in charge and show Mitchell that this failure wasn't his.

"No service here," said Pa'ali. "I'll take you to the office." The foreman pressed his bulk into a mud-covered pick-up and propped a beefy arm up in the open window.

Tomoa climbed behind the wheel of the SUV, hoping his face wasn't as red as it felt.

Mitchell buckled his seatbelt and repositioned the AC vents to blow on his flushed face. Sweat stains bled out from under his tie. "I thought this was the cool season."

"Hot and cool are relative," Tomoa said, putting the SUV into drive. Despite his wool suit coat and silk tie, Tomoa's burnished-copper skin was dry. To his chagrin, eleven years away from Vatua wasn't long enough to take the tropics out of his blood.

He followed Pa'ali's pick-up through the muck. Only forty-eight hours ago, the first vertical I-beams of the luxury resort's main tower had been in place, and stockpiles of timber and heavy equipment had covered the twenty acre lot. Then, overnight—this was the kind of thing that derailed careers, and Tomoa had worked too hard to get to where he was in Landtel. For the past three years, he had logged eighty hour work weeks and quarterly trips to the south Pacific to keep this project on deadline and under budget.

Now Landtel needed someone to blame.

"What do you know about this Pa'ali?" Mitchell asked.

"He's our general contractor's man on the ground," Tomoa said, but he sensed that wasn't the answer Mitchell was fishing for. "I don't know him or his family. Vatua's not that small." It still prickled Tomoa when people thought he should know everyone on Vatua simply because he had been born there. "You don't think much of his tidal wave story."

"No evidence of a tidal wave."

"Unless you consider three thousand tons of machinery swept out to sea no evidence."

"A tsunami of that size would have registered on the international warning system," Mitchell said. "Even if it hadn't registered—which couldn't happen—why did it only hit our construction site? Every other property around here looks fine. And where are the dead fish? The debris? It doesn't add up."

"So he's lying?"

Mitchell shrugged. "Until we find the equipment sitting on the bottom, there are simpler explanations."

Tomoa wasn't sure he believed the tsunami story either, but if it was sabotage as Mitchell had suggested back in Seattle, someone had gone to extraordinary lengths to make it look like a natural disaster. Yet, if successful, Vatua would open a lucrative, virgin business market. With so much at stake, who knew what a competitor might be willing to do.

Pa'ali's pick-up stopped next to a rectangular slat wood shack built at the edge of a white sand beach. On the shack's door, nearly lost in a skin of dirt, was the crimson Landtel logo.

Tomoa parked next to the truck. "So what happened?" he asked.

"Too soon to speculate," Mitchell said, "but that's what I'm here to find out, isn't it?" He climbed out into the heat.

Inside the construction office, a cool ocean breeze rattled through the window louvers. A fax machine sat on a rusted-metal desk. Next to the fax's handset, someone had scrawled several phones numbers with a red felt tip marker.

Mitchell nudged at one of a dozen seashells lining the window sill. An egg-shaped one with brown mottling tumbled off.

Pa'ali caught it before it hit the ground. "Cowry shell," he said, returning it to its place. "Abalone. Trochus." He pointed to each as he named it.

"You know a lot about sea shells," Mitchell said.

"Not really." Pa'ali pointed to the phone. "It's international—"

"I know." Tomoa picked up the handset.

"Why don't we wait outside," Mitchell said. He led Pa'ali out and closed the door.

Tomoa licked his dry lips. What was Pa'ali going to tell Mitchell? he wondered. He almost returned the handset to its cradle, but he had to check in with headquarters.

Even though it was Sunday in Seattle, Tomoa was not surprised when the vice-president in charge of Pacific development answered. five minutes later, orders slid from the fax. Tomoa reviewed them, then stuffed the paper deep into his pocket.

* * *

Outside, Pa'ali husked a coconut on a nail protruding from the side of the building. Mitchell leaned against the slat boards, hugging the shade and listening to the man speak.

"There is a story about the coconut," Pa'ali said, as he chopped the husked coconut in two with a single sweep of a rusty machete. The sweet water splattered onto his dark skin and ran in glistening rivulets. The rime of white coconut meat glistened. "A young girl goes searching in the ocean for food to feed her mother and young sisters. She has no brothers to do this. No father. One day, the god Kanaloa sees her leaving the ocean with nothing to eat."

Tomoa leaned on the rickety railing and pursed his lips. He started to say something, but Mitchell raised a finger, quieting him. Perhaps Mitchell thought he was getting close to something, but it sounded to Tomoa like he was getting another of Vatua's many legends.

"Kanaloa changes into a beggar, for he is a trickster and can take many forms. Every day for a week, he visits her. Each time he is impressed by her kindness, because she feeds him the awa she would have drunk herself." With quick, precise strokes, Pa'ali shaved the coconut meat. "On the eighth day, Kanaloa reveals himself and commands her to cut off his head and bury it. Reluctantly she obeys, and the next morning, on the spot where she buried Kanaloa's head, is the first coconut tree." Pa'ali presented Tomoa a piece of coconut meat on the tip of the machete. "She and her family never go hungry again."

Tomoa frowned at the flecks of rust speckling the otherwise stark white meat. "Does Nakuli still live in Hanumoa?"

Pa'ali looked hurt by Tomoa's refusal of his offering. He ate the coconut from the end of the machete. "She does," he said. "I will take you to her."

* * *

"You know this Nakuli?" Mitchell asked as Tomoa turned the SUV onto the paved road.

"She is stuck in the past." Tomoa said. "She wants to keep everyone in grass huts and shell necklaces."

Mitchell arched an eyebrow.

Tomoa groaned. "And she's my aunt."

A snore rose up from the back seat.

Tomoa adjusted the rearview mirror to check on Pa'ali. The foreman's head slumped against the closed window. The fat around his face and neck had settled into fleshy rolls.

"What was with that story about chopping someone's head off and growing a coconut tree out of it?"

Tomoa shook his head. "It's just a story."

"This Kanaloa, he's one of the local gods?"

"He's the protector of many Polynesian people," Tomoa said, "the god of the deep ocean and things that are hidden. The Maori have Tangaroa; the Samoan's Tagaloa. He's Ta'aroa in Tahiti and Tangaloa in Tonga. They're all the same, basically. It's just superstition."

"So then this Kanaloa isn't our culprit?" Mitchell smiled wryly.

Tomoa's face grew warm.

The forest thinned as the road skirted the edge of a narrow bay. On the opposite shore, the old colonial buildings and tin shacks of Pale'maka'a, the island's capital, baked under the late afternoon sun.

Near the port, they slowed to a crawl. Workers crowded the street as the afternoon shift change neared completion. Vans and small public buses wove through the congestion, stopping seemingly anywhere to pick up passengers.

"This is crazy," Mitchell said.

Forklifts hauled pallets stacked high with tinned fish bound for Sydney. Cranes loaded containers filed with phosphate mined from the outer guano islands onto a Chinese-flagged cargo ship.

"Third world progress," Tomoa said. "All this for a dollar five an hour."

The low cost of labor and the lack of significant regulations had put Vatua near the top of Landtel's site list. Tomoa's pitch for the island had led to its selection over Fatu Hiva and Tomoa's promotion to project manager.

The traffic crept forward, and eventually Pale'maka'a was behind them.

The road narrowed as it climbed into the interior of the island. Dense jungle over-arched the cracked pavement. As the sun slid into the sea, Tomoa turned on the SUV's headlights. The road dropped back down to the coast on the opposite side of the island and they rounded a rocky headland to find two-dozen buildings huddled in the gloaming on a flat of land, backed by steep cliffs and fronted by a dark sea striped with parallel lines of white breakers.

Pa'ali stirred in the back seat as Tomoa pulled in next to Hanumoa's church.

Pa'ali led them straight to Nakuli's house. His rap on the door echoed off the dark.

The door cracked. "Tomoa?" A hand motioned for them to enter. "The door, close it so the mosquitoes do not get in."

Nakuli set her kerosene lamp on a low table. The rattan chair creaked as she settled into it. She adjusted her robe to cover her thick knees and motioned for the three to sit.

Nakuli's dark eyes lingered momentarily on Pa'ali at one end of the rattan couch, passed quickly over Mitchell in the middle, and stopped on Tomoa. Her thick eyebrows pinched together.

"I saw your mother this afternoon, nephew. Odd she would not mention your return. Why do you dishonor her?" she asked.

"I don't dishonor her."

The couch trembled as Pa'ali leaned forward to look around Mitchell. "Show respect for your aunt," he said. "She has earned it."

"It is okay," Nakuli said.

Tomoa shifted uncomfortably on the couch. "This trip was... unexpected," he said. He had not intended to visit his mother, but he also did not intend to admit that to his aunt.

Nakuli's gaze shifted to Mitchell. "You are here because you think I did it."

Tomoa found his aunt's directness refreshing. Unlike westerners, Vatuans had a roundabout way to their conversation that he now found frustrating—it made getting things done a slow process.

"In a way I did," Nakuli said.

"You did?" Tomoa said.

Nakuli smiled, showing teeth stained red with betelnut. "I climbed through the forest of our ancestors to where the river gurgles over the rounded black stones spit from the belly of the world. There I collected eight sets of eight, all just the right size and breathing with the mana of Papatuanuku, the earth mother. With them, I built an altar where the sea foam lapped against it when the sun touched the water. I left a cowry shell and a bowl of awa as offerings to Kanaloa. For eight days I fasted and chanted the songs that reach back to the sea before our islands were pulled from the bottom by Rongo's great fishhook. Kanaloa saw the purity of my intentions. He came, and he took it all away."

Tomoa rubbed his gritty eyes, trying to ease his blossoming migraine. As a child he had sat at his aunt's feet and listened to her weave stories of gods and history. Auntie Nakuli had made his world come alive with the ancient magic of Kanaloa, Lono, Tane, and Rongo, but they were just stories.

Tomoa sat forward and spoke, his tone measured and rational. "Auntie, this resort will be good for Vatua. It will bring jobs and money."

"It brings those who do not understand our ways."

"No, no, auntie." Tomoa took the woman's wrinkled hand into his own. "We will not be like the others. The good we bring will outweigh the bad. We will have programs to teach the tourists about our island—"

Nakuli smiled at him as if he were still four-years old. "You will have fire dances and pretty young girls in grass skirts. You will give them Disneyland."

Tomoa's ears burned. The initial concept designs were just as she had described, and Tomoa's suggestions had, to this point, gone unheeded.

"Vatua is a place where family and village still have meaning," Nakuli said. "It's a simple place where you can look out at the ocean when the sun drops and hope that it rises again tomorrow."

"Auntie, it can be more."

"What makes you think you have that to give, Tomoa?"

"I—" Tomoa's mouth hung open.

Nakuli pushed herself to her feet. "I am an old woman, and I am tired. It is a long drive back to Pale'maka'a. You will stay here."

Tomoa started to decline, but he caught himself. Offering hospitality on Vatua was not a formality that was expected to be declined. To refuse her would be rude. He would embarrass himself and Landtel.

* * *

Tomoa slept on a futon mattress on the floor of the living room. Wind carried the subtle scent of night-blooming jasmine through the open louvers. A gecko the size of his hand startled him as it danced across the window glass in pursuit of termites. It stopped in the middle of the window and chirped defiantly. So much noise and life here, compared to the sterile quiet of his Seattle apartment. He felt eight-years old again, lost in the warmth of the humid nights.

When had Vatua become too small and backwards for him?

Restless, Tomoa rolled onto his stomach. His feet hung off the edge of the short mattress and his toes scraped on the rough wooden floor. He let the night chorus chase all thoughts from his head, and within minutes, his breathing slowed to match the rhythm of the breaking surf.

* * *

The next morning, Tomoa found Nakuli alone in the kitchen. She fed him pomelo from her garden, its tartness offset by sunset-orange slivers of sweet mango. She poured him tea from a porcelain pot.

Nakuli sat opposite him, her floral robe pulled tightly about her to ward off the morning chill. "The world is as it is because of Kanaloa," she said. "The oceans are his ink sac, and the islands are his gift. Many of the young have forgotten his name, even as he lives within their hearts."

"Those are just stories, Auntie."

"Aren't stories the history of who we are? Our stories teach us about the duality of the world. The ocean has the sky. For every fish in the sea, there is a plant on land. Kanaloa is lord of the deep, the wild and the hidden, yet he walks the world with his brother Tane, lord of the sky and all that we see on the surface of the world. There is duality within us all, and we must find balance and harmony in that conflict."

Tomoa sipped the tea. Its delicate warmth spread through his body.

"Does it matter if Kanaloa took your machines or not?" she asked.

Tomoa set his tea cup down. It did matter, he thought; how could it not?

Outside, a cacophony of bird song nearly drowned out the booming surf. Through the kitchen window, Tomoa watched children playing tag in the schoolyard next to the church. He had been one of those kids, not long ago. Unlike most, he had earned a scholarship to an American university and escaped to find prosperity elsewhere. He had resented that he had not been able to find prosperity in Vatua. That was his dream: prosperity and home ...together.

"They are still too young to know what they are losing," Nakuli said, gazing at the children.

"I don't see it that way, Auntie. Places change," Tomoa said. "People must change with them or be left behind."

Nakuli cradled her tea cup in her hands. "You are right, nephew," she said. "Places change and they must, but change should come like the seasons, not the typhoon. Then no one gets left behind, and we move forward as a people."

He finished his tea while watching the children. After several minutes, the morning bell rang and the children scattered like schools of fish into their classrooms.

"Tell me where the machines are."

"I have told you already. Kanaloa came and took them. They

are in the sea." Nakuli set her cup down. "If you must see them to believe, go find Kimo. He will know."

* * *

At the water's edge, the road ended at a small shack with a tin roof and sagging plywood walls held erect by angled two-by-fours. It had no door or windows, just holes in the walls through which the ocean breeze whistled like breath across an open bottle worn smooth by the sea.

"This is a waste of time," Tomoa said after finding no one home. In hindsight, he could not believe he had thought this a good idea. It made him look foolish.

"If this Kimo is supposed to know where the equipment is, then it isn't a waste of time," said Mitchell.

"He will come in his time," Pa'ali said. The foreman stood inside the shack to escape the late morning sun, but crescents of sweat stained the armpits of his shirt.

Tomoa sorted through a pile of faded beer cans with his foot. "I think we should contract an oceanographic study to disprove the possibility of a rogue wave. In the meantime, we can focus on a criminal investigation. No one can hide that much machinery for long, especially on Vatua." Tomoa looked pointedly at Pa'ali.

Mitchell righted a discarded paint bucket, and sat in the shade of a palm tree. "What's the rush?"

"Every day we delay is costing Landtel more money. Eventually they'll pull the plug."

Mitchell wiped his brow with his monogrammed handkerchief. He casually folded it and returned it to his pocket. "Simply moving forward doesn't guarantee you get where you want," he said. "Sometimes you just get more lost."

Tomoa's foot paused in chasing beer cans. What did Mitchell mean?

Pa'ali emerged from the shack. "He's coming."

Kimo came in an old boat with a slender mast and patchwork sail. His crown of white hair shimmered like mother-of-pearl. He pulled the boat high onto the beach behind the shack and tied it off to the trunk of a palm tree. Without a word, he collected a string of fish from the bow and sat on the sand.

With the backside of a knife, he sent fish scales dancing through the sunlight. He flipped the fish around and deftly cleaned and cut them into thin strips that he spread across a piece of driftwood to dry.

When he had finished, he looked up at the three men. "I know where. Come."

"In that?" Tomoa pointed at the boat.

"I'll go," Mitchell said, removing his shoes.

"Then I'm coming, too." Tomoa handed his shoes to Pa'ali, saying, "Wait for us here."

Kimo pushed the boat into deeper water, then jumped over the gunwale. Slowly he maneuvered through the harbor, past fleets of Taiwanese fishing boats. As they passed a point of land at the harbor mouth, he turned the boat southwest. The sail billowed as it caught the wind.

The bow peeled the ocean aside in crisp lines of foam. A flying fish burst from the water and skimmed fifty yards across the surface before diving back into the sea. Every time the bow dipped into a wave, spray leaped up and soaked Tomoa. He removed his wet shirt and let the sun warm his copper skin and the traditional Vatuan tattoo that covered his left shoulder and upper arm.

Tomoa watched the reef slide under him. He had spent his childhood on reefs like these, but still he was awed by their intricate expanse. Patches of colorful coral and bright white sand formed a quiltwork that stretched as far as he could see. Bright fish flitted among coral heads the size of delivery trucks.

Thirty minutes after leaving the harbor, they rounded a headland. A Taiwanese longliner cruised by, its hull low in the water. Its wake nearly swamped Kimo's boat.

"What are they catching?" Mitchell asked above the snap of canvas.

"Tuna and shark fin," Kimo said, before Tomoa could answer.

They sailed into a wide bay filled with a labyrinth of turquoise shallows and coral bommies. Kimo guided them through narrow channels. As they neared the shore, Tomoa recognized the project site—a muddy scar of red dirt bulldozed out onto the reef to form a platform of virgin land. The fill had been necessary because Vatua's narrow coastal plain was backed by a razor's edge of basalt.

Kimo furled the sail and allowed the boat's momentum to carry them. He moved to the bow and picked up a large stone tied off to a length of coconut fiber rope. Kimo tossed it overboard and let the line feed out, before tying it off to a crusty white cleat.

As the boat slowed, the blur of color became distinct purple tabletop corals and thickets of branching green staghorn. Then Tomoa saw it: the crimson Landtel logo on the up-facing side of a bulldozer. Dump trucks, cranes, and cars littered the bottom like children's toys.

The strength bled from Tomoa's body, and he slumped into the bottom of the boat, his back to the gunwale. They were too far off shore for someone to have easily dumped the machines here. A tsunami was the only explanation. If it happened once, it could happen again. Landtel would not be willing to take that chance. They would kill the project.

Kimo sat in the stern, threading a line through a spoon-shaped object about a foot long. A fist-sized cowry shell and a similar-sized piece of lead were wired to opposite sides of the wooden spoon. On the handle, two sharpened bamboo prongs projected at an angle away from the wood and toward the shell.

Mitchell watched intently as the old man's hands deftly tied intricate knots.

"He'e. Octopus," said Kimo, as if nothing more were needed.

With a plunk, the lure dropped over the side and settled to the bottom.

"The ancestor of my people was Rangi, who came from far across the great water. Like me, he was a fisherman. He worshiped Kanaloa, master of the great deep."

Kimo pulled on the line and then let it sink again. The lure bounced in a patch of sand near a large coral head.

"One day, Rangi was blown far from his home and got lost. For eight days he drifted. Each day he prayed to Kanaloa to bring him safely home. On the eighth day, Kanaloa took pity on him."

The lure jumped and moved side to side at the same time. The complexity of its movement belied Kimo's gentle tugging.

"Kanaloa took his favorite form of a great he'e and seized Rangi's hook. Rangi could not land him so he hung on with all his strength as the he'e swam toward the rising sun. Kanaloa dragged Rangi across the great ocean for eight days before he came to this beautiful island and these plentiful reefs."

The lure spun rhythmically, a solitary dancer looking for a partner.

Kimo waved an encompassing hand. "These reefs are good for octopus. We call this one the Octopus Garden. Kanaloa lives here, the one who stopped you. Many have forgotten him, but he lives deep within the heart of every Vatuan. He gives to his people with his own."

"Like that story about the girl and the coconut," Mitchell said.

Kimo smiled, his toothless gums stained red from betelnut. Something caught his attention and he pointed down into the turquoise water.

Barely visible because of its cryptic coloring, an octopus crept from a hole in the reef. As it flowed gracefully over the bottom toward Kimo's lure, its skin changed color and texture to match the bottom.

"He'e are masters of hiding. They can be anywhere, be anything, but they are drawn to the cowry shell. That is their weakness. Once I catch, he will become the flesh to feed my flesh."

The octopus slid away from the coral onto the sand. Its tentacles flowed around it like a living pinwheel. Then it was a blur, so fast that Tomoa did not see it move; only where it started and where it finished.

The muscles in Kimo's arms and neck stretched as he pulled sharply up on the cord, driving the barbs of the lure into the octopus. Line slid through his calloused fingers.

Below, ink billowed like a roiling thunderhead.

The old man struggled with the line and his balance. "It has the bottom. Help me."

Mitchell backed away, nearly falling in the water pooled in the boat's stern.

Kimo grunted. The tendons in the back of his hand stood out like taut cords.

Using the gunwales for support, Tomoa joined Kimo in the stern. The rough cord cut into his hands as he pulled it, but he did not let go.

Together they fought, giving slack and then pulling. Within minutes, Tomoa's muscles burned.

Tomoa forgot about everything but the line in his hands. It was not monofilament, but coconut fiber, woven in the ancient way until it was strong. His strength began to ebb. He sensed Mitchell watching him, and out of the corner of his eye, he saw the older man huddled in the bow, the sleeves of his damp shirt and trouser legs rolled up. Tomoa felt absurd, and nearly threw his hands up.

Suddenly the line pulled sharply upward and continued to come. Tomoa laughed as he hand-over-handed the line into the boat.

Kimo reached overboard and retrieved the lure. The octopus grabbed onto the gunwale, locking one long tentacle around a cleat and another around Kimo's tanned wrist. It was the largest octopus Tomoa had ever seen, easily six feet long. It must have weighed over a dozen pounds.

The octopus pulled itself free from the bamboo barbs and slithered toward the side. Two arms dangled over.

Tomoa lunged, nearly capsizing the boat. The octopus oozed through his fingers like rubbery gelatin. Three tentacles wrapped around his arm. Suckers pulled at his skin.

Kimo peeled two arms from the gunwale, the suckers popping like firecrackers as they came free. He reached for his knife.

A cold arm slithered along Tomoa's shoulder toward his neck. He slapped at it with his free hand, but the octopus slid up his arm onto his shoulder. He pushed at the gelatinous body, exposing its eyes and beak, fine chiseled like a pair of knives. "Get it—"

The boat rocked as Mitchell moved to helped. Tomoa slipped in the puddle of water and fell, cracking his elbow painfully on the boat bottom.

Kimo tried to get an angle with his knife, but gave up.

"Bite it," Kimo said, fingering a spot between the octopus' eyes and its beak.

Mitchell pulled at the tentacles, but as quickly as one came free, it would reattach to Tomoa's back or neck.

"Bite it," Kimo said again. "Like the old way."

Tomoa closed his eyes so tight he saw white not black. His teeth bore down on the rubbery flesh. The salt made his mouth water.

Memories of catching his first octopus flooded his head. His father had showed him how to bite the octopus to cripple it, and he had explained how this first octopus was how Kanaloa passed his mana to his children. Tomoa remembered the power he had felt that day.

The octopus shifted its arm from Tomoa's neck and tried to pull away. Tomoa grabbed it with both hands and bit harder.

The flesh parted and eight arms went limp.

Tomoa lay back on the bottom of the boat. His head spun in an adrenaline haze.

Mitchell sat next to him, looking concerned. Unable to speak, Tomoa raised his hand to try and tell him he was okay.

Kimo took the octopus and cleaned it. He removed the beak and skillfully strung the two halves onto a length of twine. He pressed it into Tomoa's hands.

Tomoa squeezed the octopus beak in his trembling hands. His blood darkened the twine.

* * *

"Did you find it?" Pa'ali asked as the boat's bow hit the sand.

"It's all out there," Mitchell said, putting his shoes back on.

Pa'ali grunted, sounding vindicated.

Tomoa watched Kimo push his boat back into the water and raise the sail. The old man smiled his toothless grin; then turned toward the sea.

"Are we done here?" Mitchell asked. "We should call Seattle."

"And tell them what?" Tomoa asked. He was sure they would kill the project.

Mitchell climbed behind the wheel of the SUV. The vehicle dipped as Pa'ali squeezed into the back seat.

Tomoa slipped into the passenger seat. He felt numb. "Are you going to recommend relocating to Fatu Hiva?"

"It's not my decision," Mitchell said without looking at him.

Tomoa knew that it wasn't Mitchell's decision, but his opinion carried weight—more than Tomoa's opinion ever would.

How could their pre-site surveys have missed the risk of a tsunami? "It still doesn't add up," he mumbled.

"Hmm?"

"The tsunami. Like you said earlier, it doesn't add up."

"Three-thousand tons of equipment add up," Mitchell said. He slowed as they neared the port.

"We can get oceanographic and engineering teams to figure this out." Tomoa said, thinking aloud more than anything else. "There has to be a design fix." Tomoa shook his head, uncertain. Maybe Nakuli was right and the resort was too big a step and something smaller and more integrated into Vatua's landscape would be better. If they built something more modest, they could relocate to a smaller property. Tomoa did not think Landtel would go for it—the profit margin would not be what they wanted. The large resort was the only way Tomoa could bring opportunity to Vatua.

Mitchell turned the SUV down the gravel road to the project site. He pulled in next to Pa'ali's muddy pick-up. The engine died, clicking as it cooled. "Is this right?" Mitchell asked.

Tomoa was sure it was the right place, but the construction office was gone. In its place, water lapped against a pile of river-smoothed stones a few feet high. Tomoa looked to the back seat, but Pa'ali had already climbed out of the vehicle.

Tomoa climbed out and approached the pile of stones. Sitting atop the altar, a fist-sized cowry glinted in the setting sun. In the shell's polished surface, Tomoa barely recognized himself.

Pa'ali stood at the edge of the ocean. The water ran up around his feet, his body silhouetted by the coral and orange sky.

Tomoa barely noticed when Mitchell drew up next to him. "I grew up in a small Texas town," the older man said. "My father ran a hardware store. He wanted me to take it over when he retired, but I wanted nothing to do with it. When I got my first job with Landtel, he was disappointed. I tried to explain that I helped to build things, just like he did. He looked me in the eye and said, 'I help people build homes and lives, not corporate bank accounts.' You know what? He was right to an extent, but things can change."

"Landtel will never support smaller profits."

"Landtel supports profits, period. Now tell me what you really think Vatua needs."

Had he heard Mitchell right? At this point did it matter? Tomoa's hands trembled. It did matter, and he had some ideas.

The ocean waves rumbled as a small set broke on the beach. Pa'ali had walked into deeper water, where he stopped and turned.

The light must have played tricks with Tomoa's eyes, because Pa'ali looked different. His massive bulk had slimmed and his arms seemed to elongate and hang down into the water. Pa'ali's body twisted, softened, as if the bones were dissolving away. From his torso, flaps of skin lengthened into four more suckered appendages. A bulbous head slid gently beneath the surface leaving only ripples.

Tomoa dug into his pocket, searching for the fax from Landtel headquarters. Instead of the paper with the crisp Landtel logo across its top, he pulled out a handful of sand, small shells, and fragments of sparkling white coral. The sand and coral bled through his fingers in thin streams, until only the eight tiny cowry shells were left.

Gently he slipped them back into his pocket.

Before him, the water shimmered like a sliver of Nakuli's sweet mango.

Three-Hearted

Elizabeth Twist

Bold first saw the interloper on a day when the sky was slate grey and the ocean so rough that everything stirred, even the sands of the shallow bay. Bold noticed him because the faint trace the interloper left behind tasted like Brash, Bold's twin and egg-cluster mate who sang to her before they were born.

Bold swam toward the interloper to better taste the water, but Brash's flavour faded and she tasted wrong things: glass, metal. An inside-out blood taste: not her sister, but some male outsider eight-arm. The interloper sped away before Bold could reach him. For the rest of the day, Bold sang Brash's song and recalled memories of their time together in the cluster. She sang the greater song of their tribe, the song that always sang in her heart, of the Boundless, renowned for their bravery and ferocity. Despite the ocean's turbulence, Bold was smooth inside.

The interloper returned after Bold caught the big crab. As she crunched its carapace, tiny pieces floated away. She kept four arms free to pluck these morsels from the water, moving in an elaborate dance of joy and feasting. She reached out to snatch one fat piece, only to find it gone.

She rolled her eyes. The interloper hovered nearby. He slid one arm up to his mouth and chewed the piece of crab he'd stolen.

Bold took the posture of outrage, transforming into a rigid black spiral. Her less impulsive siblings might have chosen surprise or confusion, but that was not Bold's way.

The interloper gestured back, as if oblivious to her threat. "More, please."

The insult struck a savage chord inside her. It was an affront to her and to the Boundless tribe, something she must put down. The interloper was as good as dead. She attacked.

The moment she grabbed him, she knew she'd made an error. It wasn't that he fought back: he was too weak to overwhelm her with physical force. His taste, though, stabbed through to her core, like an eel shock. Worse, it tore into her mind, and the song of the Boundless spun away from her. She was separate, alone. Sorrow pressed in.

The interloper pushed her off, gestured, "Hello, friend," and shot ink into her face.

She flailed to free herself from the chemical flavour. The interloper sped away.

For three days and nights, Bold shivered in her cave under the coral. No gesture she knew could name what she was: an ugly thing, a freak with no past. Three nights and three days crawled by before she remembered the song of the Boundless again.

* * *

Bold now hunted the interloper. She did only that which would allow her to find him and end him. She ate next to nothing, never dulling her awareness with food. She rested, but never allowed herself to drift into dream.

A day came when she caught his flavour in a nest of caves near the mouth of the shallow bay. She tasted strong metal in some places. The interloper travelled here often. She skulked in a small hole, shifting her outside to resemble rock, darkness, obscurity.

The interloper swam past, only a small distance from her hiding place. She leapt out at him, grabbed him and drew him in toward her beak. He thrashed and avoided her bite. Despair surrounded her again and she couldn't hold him.

He did not flee. "Why hate?" he gestured.

"Evil," she signed. "Taste foul. Like death."

He made the gesture for peace. "Not death. Different." He made the gesture for "Tastes good."

She'd anticipated what it would be like, touching him again. Although she could not sense the Boundless song, she knew it was there, somewhere. It would return. She put a little more distance between herself and the interloper, then moved toward him again.

"Good?" she asked.

"Good clever." He made the sign for dolphin: "Smartfish."

"Why taste like metal? Why glass?" Some eight-arms didn't know these signs, but Bold guessed the interloper did: these tastes were such an intimate part of his flavour.

Instead of answering, the interloper began to glow. A purple light surrounded and infused him. She tried to match it, but it shifted too quickly from dark to light, and she could not understand its strange intensity. She was not luminous. He shouldn't be, either.

The light surrounded her. Something drew her into a small metal and glass container. The light filled her and poured out through her arms and shone from her suction cups and she lost awareness.

* * *

When she came back into herself, she was swimming over the big coral. She moved toward her home cave, but she didn't think she would stop there. She didn't care for the cave any more. It made no difference where she slept or where she went.

Somehow the interloper had separated her from the Boundless. She now knew that an invisible mesh tied the Boundless to a common code, a way of seeing and tasting the world, a perspective that somehow limited them. The interloper had cut her free. It was nauseating.

Flashes of memory came to her: seven-armed fleshy blobs, hard at their core, grabbed her and pinched her in the place of light, metal and glass. Some creatures there were longer, slender, and had only three arms. These shocked her when they touched her.

She shook the memories off and carried on looking for something, she didn't know what.

In the distance a fellow eight-arm swam. At first she imagined it was the interloper. She rushed toward him. She would kill him, or maybe ask more questions. Questions. Demands. She'd never had those before.

A need to know.

She gripped the eight-arm, who had not seemed to sense her approach. The taste was not metal and glass, but warm and familiar, like her former self.

She released the eight-arm. "Brash?" she gestured.

"Sick," her sister gestured, turning pale lavender. "Bold, taste like a stranger," she gestured.

"No stranger, Sister," Bold signed, making the gesture for cluster mates.

"Far travel," signed Brash, indicating that Bold had crossed some unimaginable threshold.

"Yes."

"Changed," Brash said.

Bold repeated the sign for cluster mates.

Brash filled the water with fear and threat.

"Yes," said Bold.

They clashed, arms tangling. Brash's colour shifted from lavender to red-black. Bold's colour did not change, but remained the sandy beige and brown of the ocean floor. Brash's attacks were desperate, earnest, and ineffective. She bit to wound, not to kill. Bold deflected her attacks with almost no effort. She punctured the mantle over and over with her beak. Brash spasmed twice and went limp.

Bold dragged her sister back to the cave, Brash's delicate organs trailing behind her. She ate most of the corpse. What remained she hid under a rock in the corner. In former times, she would never have kept dead food in her cave: she would have considered it dirty, unnatural. The corpse flavour in the water would have sickened her.

Now she wanted that flavour. She needed to soak in it, to understand, absorb, as though she could recapture what was lost.

What was lost, yes.

Bold understood all at once. Brash attacked her for the same reason she had attacked the interloper. There were all these splits inside her now. One part of her held the past, when she and Brash were twin children of the Boundless, and all the Boundless were always with her. Now, even with Brash inside her and all around her, she could not unite with them. Then there was the fact that both these things were true at the same time. This she knew in the middle of her, somewhere between her three hearts.

She wondered if smartfish felt this way. How could they stand it? The world opened to her, unfolded, split after split, relentlessly. She thought she would burst.

She stayed in the cave for a long time. Although it rotted, she still ate Brash's body. She couldn't stand for it to go to waste.

* * *

The interloper came many days later. His glass and metal flavour had faded. Bold thought maybe she couldn't detect it because she tasted that way too.

"I came to see how you are," he said.

She wasn't sure how he said it. His gestures were subtle, perfunctory. To her surprise she knew what he meant. He used something more than the symbolic gestures of the Boundless, the show-me-how-you-did-that give and take.

For the first time since she'd eaten Brash, something excited her.

"How are you?" the interloper repeated.

She began a gestural dance, but soon abandoned it. Instead she made slight movements and subtle colour changes. She held a single idea in her centre: "I'm lonely."

To her surprise, he seemed to understand. "Yes. You are different now. Special. Smartfish."

"You did this to me."

"No. I am a conduit, a portal to them. I was the first. Now there is you."

"Who are they?"

The interloper glowed lavender at the question. Bold swam back so the light could not swallow her. The glow subsided. "The others," he said.

Images flashed in her mind, ideas from the interloper mingled with memories. Harsh, right-angled glass rooms filled with glowing water. Drifting down a corridor, and many arms, encased in a grey, tasteless barrier, reaching for her. Sharp metal points that stabbed her. A shiny ball that rolled toward her and in through one of her vents. She thought she felt it now, shifting inside her.

She fought against strong arms, tried to escape. The arms around her were the interloper's. She was not in the glowing corridor, but safe outside her cave. She relaxed a little. The interloper let her go.

"You work for these others?" She had no intention to attack; the vision had drained her energy. She needed to understand, to know what to do next.

"They made me this way. I search for those, like you, who have potential. I don't intend harm. They watch, through me, for those like you. They take them and do what they do."

"You work on their behalf."

"I don't mean to. I am lonely. Now there is you, and soon there will be more. It will happen to you too. You'll seek out those like you. You won't be able to help it."

"When?"

"Soon."

Bold tasted the interloper's loneliness. Her own isolation bloomed within her. The others had violated her, ripped her from union with the Boundless. She had no home, no tribe. She quivered a little. One thought lingered: she would find the others and tear them into pieces.

"No," the interloper said. "You must not think that. You cannot conquer these others. They are too strong. They are too smart. They have weapons. They disabled you with nothing but light. What do you think you can do against them?"

"I'm not sure."

She wanted him to stay. Speaking in the new way was better than loneliness. His hesitation and fear bothered her, though. In the end, she chased him away so she could think and plan.

* * *

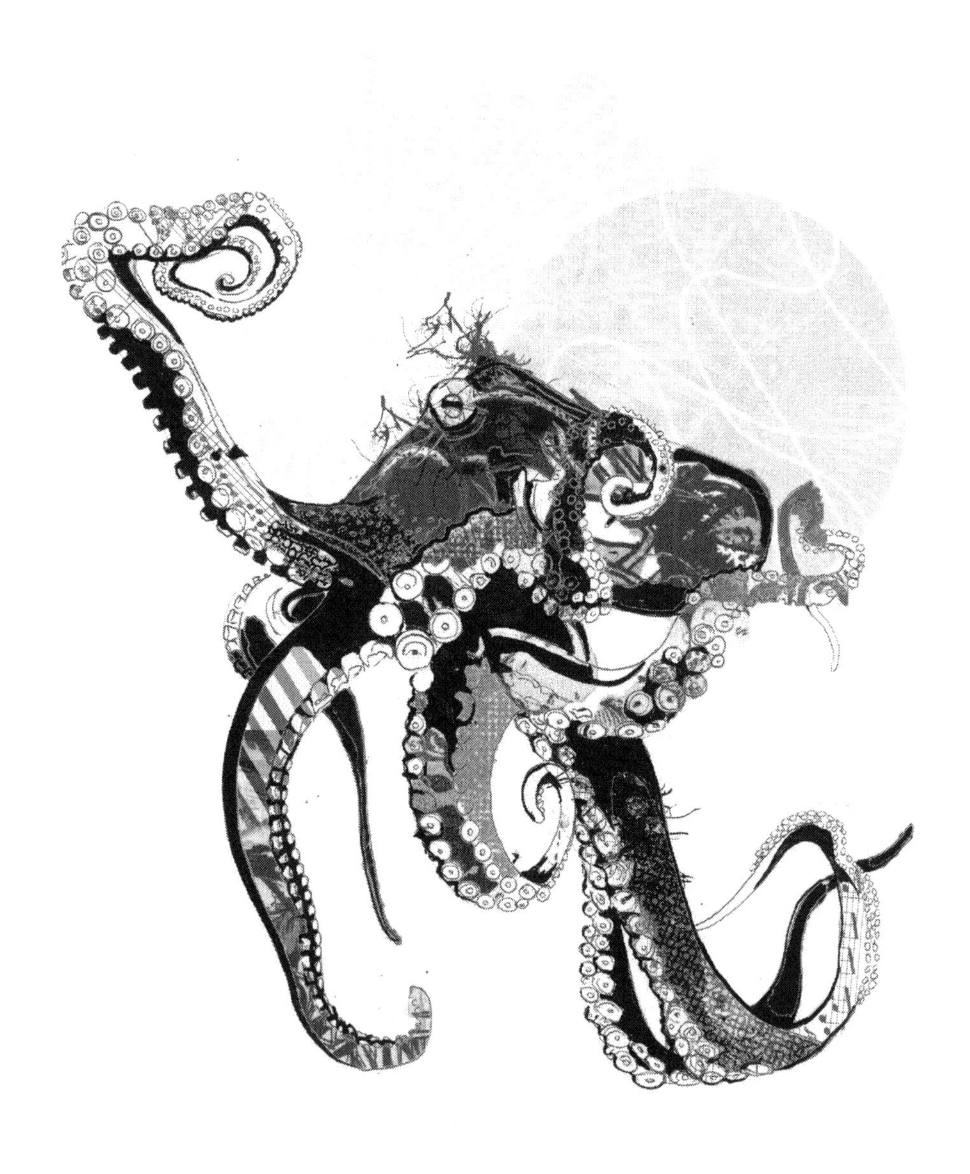

The plan was simple. Bold held it in her centre brain until it was as clear as the cool walls of the coral cave, as vital as the pulse of Mother Ocean through her vents, as fundamental as the song of the Boundless had once been.

She chased her brothers and sisters down through the reef, through the sands beyond. Each one she approached, she tasted deeply, searching for the flavour of fearlessness and bravery that once marked her.

Some were strong. She approached them with caution. She tried not to kill them if they fought. When she did kill, she ate to honour their sacrifice.

At long last, she found one who carried the flavour she sought.

"Boundless," the eight-arm signed.

She did not know him. He was no clustermate, but his greeting meant he was one of her former tribe.

Bold simplified her language, speaking in the old gestural way, so he would understand her. "Boundless," she gestured. She sang the song of the Boundless from memory. She hoped she could sing it well enough that he would trust her.

Before she'd left her cave, Bold had rolled in Brash's scanty remains, hoping that the taste of her Boundless sister would disguise her glass and metal flavour.

The stranger turned white, then bright red. Fear, and alarm. "Sick" he gestured.

"No," Bold signed. "Ate deadfish."

"Sick," he signed, turning a pale pink shade that meant good humour. "Gross."

Bold reached out with the tendril of her taste arm, and caressed him.

"What?" he gestured, showing a faint flush of sexual interest.

From deep inside her, the lavender light arose as a deep internal pressure, akin to the urge she knew would come when it was time to mate and lay eggs. Unlike children, the light would not wait on ritual or tradition. It demanded its birth now, and birthing through her, it rendered her transparent. This was better and more urgent than blending with a complex background, better than emulating rocks and coral so none could see her. She became something new: a doorway, a living passage to new life.

One thing she wanted more than anything else: for this not-stranger, this strong handsome eight-arm, to pass through to the other side. She knew if he did, he would become like her, a singer of glass and metal. Through this new tribe, glass and metal would propagate throughout all the ocean.

In this moment, the moment when the portal opened through her and inside her, Bold had a complete connection with the others. She joined with them. She shared their dream of the future.

After the glass and metal eight-arms dominated the oceans and became a new breed, a new and better kind of smartfish, they would grow hard shells and walk upon the land. There dwelled the two-legged riders on the surface, those who floated in hard metal boats.

They could be sung into metal and glass too. The dwellers on the surface were only a different sort of smartfish, Bold saw that now, and the lavender light and the portal and the glass and metal song would be to them like a fungal disease, and it would spread across the dry surface in an instant.

The seven-armed glass and metal Gods – so they saw themselves – would conquer all.

Bold was among the first. She and the interloper would lead the charge.

The stranger hovered on the portal's verge. She wanted him to go through it. The interloper had told her she would.

She grasped the stranger, drew him close, beak to beak, vent to vent.

She tore his mantle, ruining his brain and killing him.

The light winked out. She was alone.

The glass and metal seven-arms could make her want whatever they wished, but they could not control what she did. When they changed her, they made space inside her, for thought, deep memory, and dreams. She sang a new song, a song of mourning, as she rolled in the fresh corpse. She hoped, before the day was through, to kill more of the Boundless, to stop the army of metal and glass from growing any larger.

* * *

Some months later, the interloper found her again. She sat in a new cave, in a coral reef distant from where she had begun.

She desired all the time now to find eight-arms. The seven-armed singers of glass and metal barraged her smartfish mind with fantasies about their ability to convert any eight-arm. They could still be a vast army, the fantasies said. They could still conquer the world below the waves and the world above.

Bold felt in her body that a weaker eight-arm would die rather than endure the transformation. She knew the seven-arms lied. In any case, there were no eight-arms within three days' travel. She had killed most of them; the others had fled.

The interloper came whining. "No eight-arms," he said, reverting to dumbfish talk. "Help."

She slid from the cave. As she moved, a new song whispered along her skin. Not a song of glass and metal, not the song of her former tribe, but the song of the memory of the Boundless in a different key, the key of Bold.

"I'll help you," she said, "but not how you want me to help you."

"We must find eight-arms. We'll die if we don't."

She caressed him. It seemed the seven-arms sent different dreams to each of their portal creatures.

"You won't die," she told him. "You only think you will."

"I will die. I know it."

"No. How long since you caught an eight-arm?" She slipped her taste arm across his mantle. His skin shifted from white to pink, matching her coral colour and texture.

"Two, maybe three months." His skin flushed a deeper shade of pink. He began to panic again.

"Not dead yet," she said. She allowed the new song to play on her skin as she drew him in and held him close.

"No, but the warning – "

"Hush." She stroked him. "Just thoughts. Not real. Not true."

"What's real?" he said. He entwined his arms with hers.

"This."

She sang the song until he sang it too.

Vulgaris

Ives Hovanessian

Once upon a fishing village, where a dismal haze choked the horizon and the air was thick with brine, shore and sky were severed by an everpresent brume of vapor, etching a line of demarcation across the class divide.

Above the clouds, towering castles seemed to float on the billowy formations, inexplicably balancing their hefty breadth at each cliff's edge.

Down below, the stench of blood chum saturated the sand, inviting hermit crabs and gulls to feast on the decaying innards of washed-up sea life.

Untouched for centuries, the island had subsisted as a sovereign realm where mollusk and crustacean, urchin and anemone held court without mankind's mortal threat. Free from foreign dominion, the surrounding waters bred extraordinary specimens of nearly every branch of oceanic phyla, all flourishing under the watchful eye of an octopus of hulking proportions. The ghostly white cephalopod, which lived 200 feet beneath the sea in a cave resembling a chimneystack, trumped the largest *Enteroctopus dofleini* by a landslide, outweighing it by an astonishing six hundred pounds. Though despite its prodigious build, it possessed a surprisingly gentle disposition, spending the majority of its day resting in its rocky refuge, surviving only on the snails and lobsters that happened to cross its path. Following their placid ruler's graceful lead, the loyal subjects co-existed in harmony, swimming around the underwater Eden blissfully unaware of the dangers lurking just beyond their turquoise cocoon.

But as the nature of things would have it, nothing pure prevails, and before long, whispers traveled like waves to the outside world, alerting them to the phenomena taking place around the uncharted island. Without the splendor of science to back them, they speculated that a hydrothermal vent somewhere in the vicinity was responsible for the staggering growth spurt, as the life it spawned was vastly superior to the hauls they were accustomed to reeling in.

Prospectors from near and far heard the news and jumped at the chance to pillage the hidden pocket of virginal sea of its exotic treasures, sending their most skilled fishermen and divers to survey the area. Amongst their findings, the cave that housed the giant octopus emitted a hot cloud of black smoke, testing positive for unusually high levels of iron and sulfur. Furthermore, not only was the stretch fraught with life of an edible variety, but trace amounts of precious metals affirmed that a considerable fortune awaited them on the ocean floor.

Subsequent to this winning endorsement, an aquatic Gold Rush ensued. Droves of venture capitalists and members of the gentry left behind their lives on the mainland to embark on the lucrative business of mineral mining and high-priced seafood.

It was a feeding frenzy by any other name; a mad dash to be the first to milk the burgeoning alcove of its natural resources. Within days, fleets of ships assembled and set sail, carrying a select group of the region's most cutthroat tycoons and their families, bringing with them both luxury and necessity alike—architects and masons to craft their villas, teachers and nannies to rear their children, couturiers and milliners to keep them bedecked in the finest frocks. Most importantly, they conscripted a motley crew of the dregs of society to do the grunting once there. Pick pockets and drunks, rapists and ex-cons, whores and widows, all looking to get away from their sordid pasts and willing to work for next to nothing.

Baited by hope and the allure of Paradise, they packed their meager belongings and signed their lives away into indentured servitude.

* * *

Accommodations on the island were supplied in the form of lumber and nails, and expected to come together at the hands of the laborers themselves. Splintered planks and rusty spikes joined haphazardly, erecting row after row of the duplicate huts that comprised the village below the mist.

With the issue of shelter out of the way, jobs were divvied amongst them based on age, physical stature and natural faculty—the strongest and most acute assigned the more crucial tasks. The men were sent into the water to tend to the fishing and diving, while the women and children took to the shore, lining up around makeshift workstations positioned along the docks.

Under the harsh beams of the unforgiving island sun, they drew, dressed, and packed the fish, tearing through their bellies —gill to vent— pulling out the slimy entrails and tossing them into nearby barrels. The barrels, bursting from the pressure of the discarded remains, spilled over to the beaches, littering them with sharp skeletons and flaccid sheaths. From the cliffs above, the ghastly sight gave the impression of thousands of snakes that looked to have slithered out of the foam and shed their shiny, gray hides onto the wet grains.

Days and nights of toiling away in the ocean left the workers with a pungent odor they could not wash off. Their unprotected skin, desiccated from the salty sea, calloused and cracked and bled easily. Dorsal fins and glistening scales followed them everywhere they went, leaving a trail behind them lest they forgot their way.

After years of enduring the exceedingly brutal conditions of the island, the dregs began realizing the Utopia they'd been promised was nowhere to be found. Some returned to the mainland, tired of the monotonous grind; while others stayed the course, deciding stewed fish heads were better than starving back home. Still others managed to excel within their means. Those who exhibited notable work ethic were rewarded with higher rank, promoted to delegating chores to their peers.

Inspired by the entrepreneurial spirit of the magnates they served, a few saved their pennies and started businesses of their own, the most favored of which were the pubs. The dingy establishments became a haven for the dregs, who congregated around their weathered stools after tedious days of strain. But chaste as were the intentions of the fledgling bar owners, time evinced resentment and drink a perilous alchemy, fanning the flames of an overdue blaze. The village erupted into bedlam, pitting the settlers against their brethren.

And while the poor ate each other alive below the cliffs, the rich continued to get richer above them, the spoils plundered from the depths turning the wealthy families into pecuniary juggernauts almost overnight. Everything from fish and salt, coral and kelp, copper, nickel and cobalt was theirs for the taking. The tiny island was pumping out more than they could handle, forcing some of the houses to merge into mutually beneficial conglomerates to keep up with the ever-growing demand.

No one knew for sure why such abundance welled from the ocean, but many suspected that the colossal octopus could hold the key. Over time, the villagers began regarding the noble mollusk as a deity of sorts, invoking it in times of want and need. And though they ransacked every inch of the water, a pact was made to defend the tentacled God at all cost.

* * *

Francis Kinney, son of Patrick II—head of the island's pearl empire—had traveled the globe several times by the age of twenty-five, and been granted permission to leave permanently if it so pleased him. Lord Kinney had little confidence in the abilities of his eldest child, believing his younger brothers to be better suited to take over in the event of his passing.

It would have been difficult to mishandle the already thriving business. The calcium-laden bivalves did a superb job of yielding the biggest, most lustrous pearls the planet had ever seen—a favorite of droop-necked socialites everywhere—but Lord Kinney was sure Francis would find a way.

Francis wasn't especially disappointed in his father's lack of faith in him, for the pursuit of commerce had never held his interest. But he also knew he could never leave the island for good. His wanderlust was wearing thin and *she* had a tight grip on his soul.

* * *

She was an Arabian horse; wild and free and impossible to tame. Her pale skin, nearly transparent in the daylight, revealed the delicate workings of the thumping veins winding toward her unattainable heart. At night, she emitted a creamy opal glow so bright it shamed the harvest moon at perigee. Long, red hair framed her face in loose, savage curls, arching atop her head like a crown before cascading downward to meet her supple breast. Her peerless beauty brought the island to its collective knees, casting a spell over the men and rousing envy in the women.

More enchanting still was what lay beneath her pulchritudinous facade—a razor wit and agile mind, distinguishing her greatly from the rest of the aristocracy.

Francis had loved her since the day their eyes met, making every endeavor to get her to love him back. He demanded his father request a formal betrothal, sweetening the pot with a generous financial incentive. But the Pembrokes had no use for compensation, telling the Kinneys that their daughter was at liberty to do as she wished. The Pembrokes had never been ones to meddle in Abigail's affairs.

Born into an unimaginable inheritance, Abigail Pembroke had the opulence of the universe at her disposal and could not be bought with material things alone; for it was the written word that possessed her heart, and the brilliant men, whom she called "Gods and Magicians," who created it.

A voracious reader from an early age, Abigail found the waking world insufferably stale, and plunged head-first into books instead. As a young woman, she became a patron of the arts, lavishing her beloved "Conjurers of Magic" with largesse beyond their dreams. They, in turn, hailed her a muse, spinning prose like silkworms in her honor.

Though she seemed perfect in many ways, Abigail was certainly not without her faults, sharing her bed with many of the writers invited to the island on her father's dime. Scandalous rumors of her promiscuity rang throughout the ruling houses, fueling Francis' fervent ire.

Seeing his valiant efforts go unnoticed, Francis took a new approach—setting pen to paper to express his unrelenting devotion. The response it induced, however, left much to be desired…

Dearest Francis,

I must admit your colloquial dabblings are quite endearing, but I'm afraid they are no match for the gifts of my Magi. Better to leave the craft to the masters.

Oh, you silly boy, what exactly is it you're doing? Stop this nonsense at once. We have always been the best of friends. Let us not complicate things with trifling matters of the heart.

Do come to this Sunday's fête, won't you? I've arranged for Sir Lionel Brisk to read a few passages from his latest collection. His work is just divine, I'm hardly able to contain my excitement.

Amuse bouche and libations at noon on the veranda. Don't be late.

Abigail

Francis read and reread her brief missive, completely misconstruing its contents. Letters wouldn't do, he convinced himself. If Abigail were to ever return his love, he'd have to earn her respect, and he could only do so by being published.

For the next several months, he threw himself into writing, scribbling feverishly on very little sleep. He attempted them all with paltry success – poetry and essay, novel and play – all resulting in insipid, redundant tripe. Nevertheless, he sent them off to publishers, praying for a miracle.

Soon thereafter, the rejections began flowing in by the dozen. Some were kinder in tone, letting him down gently, while others were outright nasty, scolding him for squandering their time and informing him that they were uninterested in reading cold submissions from amateurs and hobbyists.

Ego bruised but will unshattered, Francis agreed that some much needed rest was in order. He'd clear his thoughts and take up again shortly, immersing himself meanwhile in the genius of others.

* * *

Dodging drunks at every corner, Francis ventured through their squalid alleys to arrive at the only bookshop in town—owned and operated by an old man who had the distinction of being the island's sole inhabitant who'd journeyed there as neither dreg nor gentry. Following the death of his wife, he'd rounded up his measly savings and abandoned their home for the serenity of the ocean.

Francis was familiar with the shop, though he'd never been inside. It was always deserted, apart from Abigail's weekly visits. She had single-handedly kept the place afloat, her insatiable lust for words bringing in its only income.

"How do they do it?" he wondered aloud to himself.

"Octopus ink," croaked a voice from behind.

Francis turned to find the old man smiling in his direction, a stack of books in hand.

"I'm sorry," he began, "I didn't mean to disturb you."

"Quite alright, my boy. I could use the company. It gets rather lonely in here. Now, what can I help you with today?"

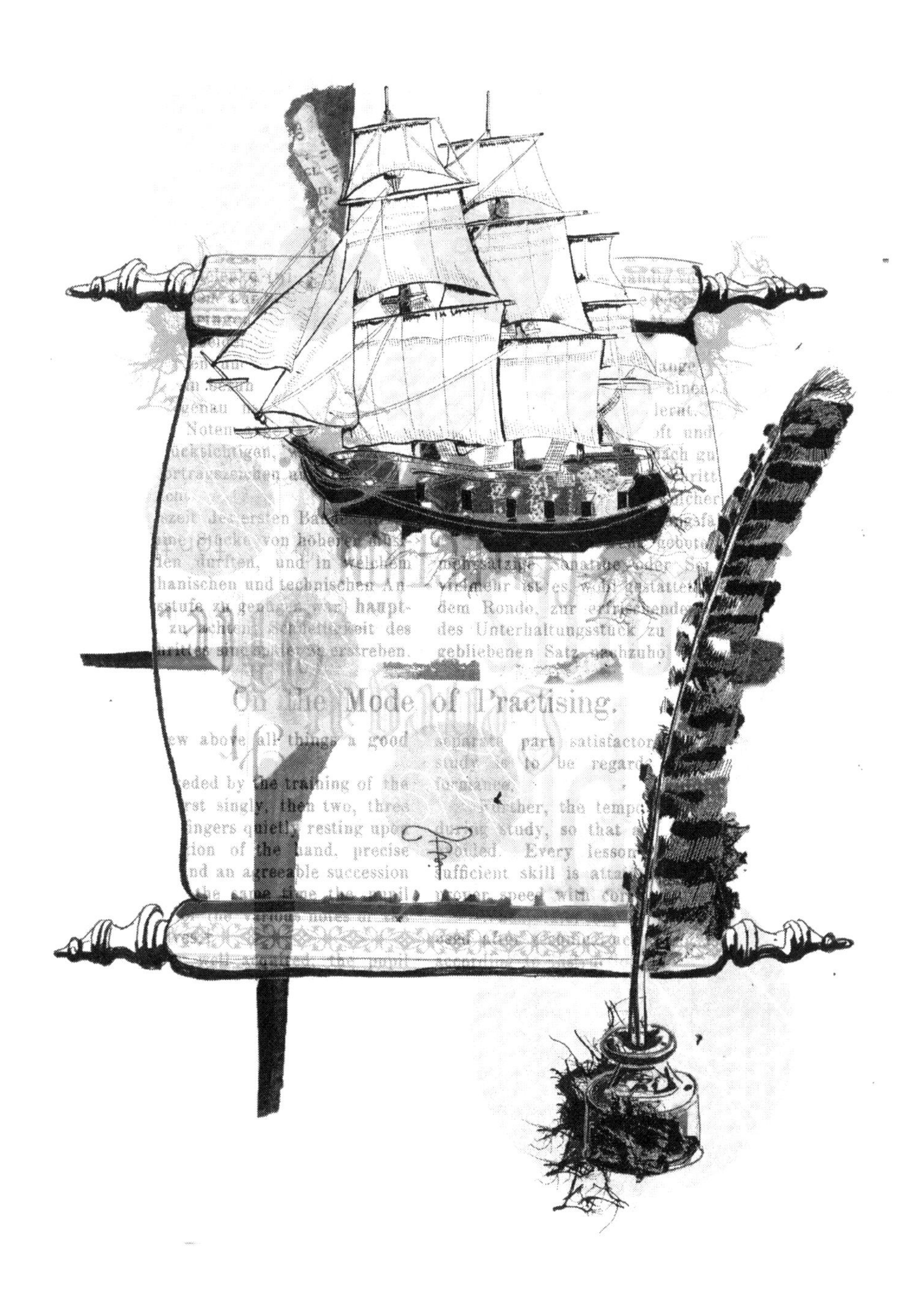
On the Mode of Practising.

"Actually, what was that you said about the octopus? Something about their ink?"

"Oh, it's nothing, really. A lovely little tale I heard as a child."

"How does it go? I'm really very interested," Francis insisted.

"Well, they say that's the big secret—the ink of an octopus. All the greats were said to have used it to draft their masterpieces."

Francis' eyes widened as he hung on every word.

"I wouldn't give it much thought. The writers themselves likely contrived the myth. Adding a bit of romance to their art. It's what they do, isn't it?"

Francis plopped down a considerable sum of money on the counter and sprinted out of the shop as quickly as his legs could carry him, a breathless '*thank you*' echoing through the swinging door.

Though uncertain and somewhat skeptical of the validity of the old man's story, he decided that it was, in the very least, worth a try. Desperation had driven him to madness and he was willing to go to the ends of the earth to win the affections of his one, true love.

* * *

Procuring an octopus would not pose a challenge; the island was brimming with them. They were everywhere, slinking around freely like feral cats. In fact, the villagers had to take care to avoid crushing them with each step, oftentimes finding their squishy suckers under their feet. But Francis surmised that, should the legend work, he'd have to sacrifice something with more consequence than the mangled remnants lodged in his shoe. And with that, he set his sights on the eight-armed king that slumbered in the deep.

Within days, a diving crew from off the coast was given their orders and an inconceivable bounty in exchange for their vows of silence and the un-ruptured ink sack and three pumping hearts of the magnificent beast.

Equipped with the necessary provisions, the men boarded a dogger boat and headed out in the dead of night. In a separate bateau, keeping a safe distance from harm, Francis led them to the top of the chimneystack peeking slightly out of the undulating tide. The octopus would surely be awake at this hour, making their quest all the more harrowing, but the mission could only be performed in the darkness, away from the prying eyes of the island.

Girded by heat resistant suits, backs heavy with regulators and tanks, the men dove in, one by one, dropping warily toward the scalding vent. They approached the crevice deliberately, their silent descent lit by the blinding rays of brass lamps. At the mouth of the cave—an oval maw more caliginous than the water around it—an enormous shadow waited, two golden discs looking out at the semi-circle forming just outside. Proceeding cautiously, an assortment of ripe bait was proffered forth, dangling at the end of a thin, metal pole. The octopus reached out a dappled appendage, moving past several offerings to the farthest swaying fish. Just as it gripped the carcass, a steel hook shot into its mottled skin, pulling the ancient creature from its broiling grotto.

Braced as they were for a vicious struggle, the men were bewildered to find that none ever came. Despite its massive bulk and strength, the octopus gave itself over to their catching snares with a strange docility, succumbing to its fate with nary a fight.

* * *

Francis Kinney locked himself in his quarters and sat down to devour the first heart.

Carving it into thin, uniform slivers, he ate them raw, without the aid of spices, dipping them only in the blood splattered around the rim of the dish. He consumed every piece, cleaning off the juices with his tongue, then reached for the ink sack lying on ice.

A large bowl placed under the pouch ensured not an ounce was wasted as he punctured the casing with a small surgical lancet. He emptied the murky fluid into a wide-mouthed basin, not bothering to transfer it to the glass inkwell on his desk.

Francis soaked the tip of a quill and wrote his first word. Instantly, his hand darted across the page without an independent thought of his own. Verse upon verse of the most devastatingly beautiful prose he'd ever read poured onto the parchment faster than his fingers could guide the plume. Unable to process the unfathomable happening, he forged on without pause, stopping only to eat the other two hearts.

The sun rose and set outside his window more times than he noticed, and by week's end the magnum opus came to a close, dotted with the very last drop of the slain king's pilfered ink. Without hesitation, Francis ran to the post, soliciting once again to the editors who'd previously shunned him; though this time, the reception was drastically different.

Right away, a bidding war commenced between the elite publishers of the industry, all vying for the exclusive rights to what they deemed THE GREATEST WORK OF FICTION EVER PENNED. Francis sold it to the most zealous amongst them, seeking—in lieu of payment—a shipment of the manuscript to the island; one for every man, woman and child.

* * *

The arrival of the books brought with it all the jubilation of a Christmas morning. Groups of villagers, dreg and noble alike, pushed each other out of the way to be first to set eyes on the monumental tome. Francis strode up and down the beach, strutting like a peacock, anticipating their reactions and thinking of a fitting speech to thank them for their praise. So certain was he that an outpouring of revelry would reverberate off the cliffs, he readied himself to cover his ears. He'd have to try to sound humble as well. No one liked a braggart, he reminded himself.

The anxious denizens began reading, burying themselves into the freshly minted text, following every line with strict attention, not wanting to miss a beat. But slowly, slowly, ever slowly, their faces took on the most peculiar shapes. From one word to the next, happy, smiling mouths and eyes melted and contorted like beeswax left by a fire. Horror and disgust replaced delight, sending Francis into a terrible confusion. He picked up a copy to see what the commotion was, immediately realizing that the words printed on the page were not his own.

"I, Francis Kinney, eldest son of Patrick and Anne, have a number of transgressions to air…"

And with that began a written confession to some of the most heinous atrocities of the century, linking Francis to the scene of every crime. Decapitation, mutilation, rape—all chronicled by the minute, gory details that only the investigators and the culprit himself could have known.

His last confession was the hardest to bear—the merciless beating and murder of Abigail Pembroke, citing jealousy and degradation as motive.

Indeed, Abigail had been murdered the night before, though her corpse hadn't turned up yet. A drunk from the alley behind the bookshop robbed, killed and stuffed her into a dumpster, hoping to walk away with a handful of shekels.

Francis couldn't understand it, but the ocean knew too well. Seemed the mighty octopus had not been so passive after all, camouflaging its ink in its moment of death, as it'd done its skin so many times in life.

The very next morning, along the cluttered shore of the island, the lifeless body of Francis Kinney hung by a hook, gutted like a fish.

Venus of the Waves

Karen Munro

Every night when I come home from work, I check the controls on the two-thousand-gallon salt-water tank in the middle of the living room. The water is fifty degrees and clear as glass. It's constantly recirculated, constantly scrubbed and adjusted and made perfect and new.

Reed watches while I make dinner. I play music—Debussy. I'm past feeling embarrassed about schmaltz.

joel, he says tonight. *do u think it ws worth it?*

"Of course." We've had this conversation before. I've never pretended not to know what he's talking about.

think about it tho

I put the knife down and look at him. He's floating beside the keyboard, his skin flushed and mottled, his slit-eyes turned to me.

"We were at the end of our rope, honey. We had to try something."

One of his arms hovers over the keyboard, weightless in the water. Then he types. *only a few years tho*

"Well, I want those years." I start chopping again. "I want you."

no leaving

"No leaving."

He drifts away from the keyboard. I pick up the knife again. I'm making minestrone, from his mother's recipe.

Later, as I'm tasting the soup, Reed goes back to the keyboard.

im not sure, he says. *i know your sure but im not*

The soup seems suddenly too salty. I put the spoon down. "What are you saying?"

The tip of his arm floats over the keyboard. He starts to press a key, withdraws, then types.

im not sure im

His typing has improved but sometimes it's still hard to understand. "What do you mean? You're not sure you're what?"

He floats. His eyelids close, longer than a blink.

me

Reed was a lovely man. A sharp-edged, brilliant, sparkling man. You could see the life in him, like bubbles rising in a glass of wine. I've kept all our old photos up around the apartment, I haven't taken anything down. I've watched him eye them, sideways to the tank wall, his siphon fluttering thoughtfully.

He had one of those wide-open faces that actors have, the kind that show every emotion. Not a lovely face, but who wants lovely? He had one snaggle tooth in the front, his English tooth he called it, even though he was from Hoboken and about as English as Clark Gable. He wore his hair long on top, so he could comb it into a sticky pompadour from time to time. He experimented with narrow moustaches, beards, sideburns.

He loved the dark joke, the unpleasant innuendo. He judged people mercilessly, he adored parties, he encouraged gossip. He gave money to bums and suffered the spiels of evangelists. He could be cruel, but he was never mean.

Most baffling of all, he loved me. For seventeen years he kept his boots under our bed, though God knows I was never much of a conquest. He saw something in me that no other man did. Maybe just a resting place, a cove. When he got sick he promised not to leave me, not if there was breath in him to fight. I never knew Reed to break a promise.

When they told us about the option to transplant, I passed quickly through shock and on to morbid curiosity. I crept away to watch videos in the hospital's hidden alcoves, my screen tipped at an angle for privacy. I'd never thought much about octopuses. Octopi. They were something for children, part of an alphabetical bestiary.

The Internet videos I found were like hardcore porn. Their loose, purplish flesh, the way they flowed endlessly in and out of tiny tubes and holes. They seemed terribly, grotesquely female.

In fact, the octopus they used for Reed was a female. Is a female. All transplant octopuses are female, because females are larger than males, and bigger is better. Fewer complications.

We never saw her before the transplant; there wasn't time, it wasn't done, and somehow it seemed gauche to press. She existed just out of our sight, beyond our ability to imagine her, unnerving. So Reed gave her a name. By that time he'd watched his own share of online videos, or maybe he remembered the real nature of octopuses better than I did. That loose, wattled, deep-purple skin, the sudden spurting emissions of inky, salty fluids. The glistening, clambering limbs. He named her Venus. Goddess of love.

They'd leave enough of her brain function to help Reed control his bewildering new limbs, parrot beak, poison barb. But while Venus would occupy some small corner of the building, Reed would hold the lease. He would still be Reed, they told us. Reed's memories, Reed's character. No reason to worry about that.

I come home from work with a bucket of live crabs from the fish market, my tie loose around my neck, my briefcase under my arm and in my hand the stack of mail that beautiful Binjamin the doorman has given me. We get bushels of mail these days—bills from surgeons and radiologists and oncologists, from therapists and phlebotomists and hematologists and all the insurance companies—and I'm distracted by the thought of all the money we still owe. It takes me a couple of minutes to check the tank.

It's empty.

I stand there, the bucket in my hand. The only sound in the apartment is the bubbling of the tank pump, and the slow scrape of claws inside the bucket. I look closer, in case he's hidden himself under the coral reef. He's gotten good at camouflage. He says it's like speaking in an accent.

He's not there. I stare into the icy, invisible water. I think: he's been stolen. I think: the cleaning woman. She did something. She put bleach in the tank. She killed him by accident and threw him in the trash.

I stare stupidly into the tank for almost a full minute. Then I turn and look around the room, and notice there are faint dark spots leading across the Berber, like footprints in dewy grass. The bathroom door is ajar.

Reed is in the bathtub, two arms wrapped around the faucet handles. No water in the tub. He looks up at me. His pupils are black slots set sideways in his eyes.

"What are you doing?" I ask.

For a moment he lies still. Then two arms rise toward me. I hesitate, then lean forward and put a hand under his sagging mantle. He's cold and soft, and so heavy I can barely lift him. Venus is a hundred pounds, easy. Maybe more. Something in my back pops when I stand.

We stagger back to the tank. The lid is ajar, no more than a few inches. Impossible to believe that he fit his whole body, fifteen feet from tip to tip, through such a tiny space.

"What were you thinking?" I ask, when he's back in the tank. He floats, unspooling vaguely. Then he reaches down to the keyboard and types.

dont know His siphon flutters. *wanted to be*

He pauses.

out

I can still feel Venus's suckers against my skin, cold and big as quarters. It occurs to me to say that we didn't invest half a million dollars so he could asphyxiate himself. I dig the heel of my hand into the pain in my lower back, and say nothing.

He closes his eyes and floats in the middle of the tank with his arms arched out from his mantle, as if he's trying to sense something. Or trying not to.

Venus is a Giant Pacific octopus, *Enteroctopus dofleini*. She's smarter than a dog, smarter than a toddler. She keeps part of her brain in her arms. With her suckers, she not only touches but tastes. She's strong enough to crush a beer keg, and she has such fine motor control that she could use a typewriter, if she saw a reason to.

"She's smarter than I am," Reed murmured, late in the game, stoned on morphine with the contracts in front of him.

The intelligence of the octopus is important, the doctors told us, because it means the body can send and receive complex signals. If you have to move a skyscraper, you don't put it in a cornfield. You put it in a city, a place that can support it. The human brain needs connections. It needs call and response, proprioception, complexity.

The size of the octopus is important, they said, because of course humans are large animals. The human brain is large. Even so, there's a bulging scar around the back of Reed's new head, which is also his body. It's dimpled and taut, like the seam on a baseball.

Finally—and this was key—the octopus is an invertebrate. The spine is one of the most delicate, complex parts of the human body. By comparison, the brain itself is simpler to handle and transport.

Quickly cauterize the part of the brain that knows the spine is damaged beyond repair, that searches for the lost links and missing impulses, and offer it instead a body with no spine at all. After a period of disorientation, responses have been extremely positive.

They didn't tell us that the Giant Pacific octopus lives only three to five years. They didn't tell us that octopuses are antisocial, that they're cannibalistic, that they mate once and then die. And somehow it was never clear to me what it would mean, that Reed wouldn't have full occupancy of his new body, but would cohabitate with something else.

In retrospect, they could have told us everything. I can't imagine we would have refused. I wanted those five years. I wanted whatever I could get. And he'd promised he wouldn't leave. Not while there was breath in him to fight.

I wake up to screaming. It's pitch black. It's the tank, I realize—the tank alarm is going off.

When I get there Reed is bright purple, jetting in circles.

"What's wrong?" I hit the emergency button and the alarm shuts off. Quiet falls, except for the bubble of the recirculating pump.

Reed doesn't stop swimming. I trot back and forth with him, tapping on the tank wall.

"Reed, honey. Do you need a doctor?" There was the possibility of a spontaneous rejection. We thought the time for that was past, but maybe it's happened anyway. My glasses, my phone—

He streaks back to the keyboard and starts typing, using three arms instead of his usual one. The device stutters.

thought i wasnthere thought i was inthesea

I squint to read. My heart is drumming in my throat and ears. I'm too old and fat to be running around in the middle of the night.

"Jesus Christ. Are you telling me you had a dream? And you pressed the panic button?"

Reed hesitates.

"Reed," I say. "Are you all right?"

yes

"You're not hurt?"

no

"Why did you ring the bell?"

He lifts his arms away from the keyboard, up around his eyes. He seems to be looking at his own arms with a kind of panic.

thought i was

I wait.

inthesea, he types quickly, then pulls his arm back as if he's afraid of the keyboard.

"You thought you were in the sea," I repeat. "Well, you're not. You're at home. Okay?"

We stare at each other. Then he surges to the wall in front of me and spreads himself against it, flattening his mantle and spreading his arms as if he's trying to embrace me. His suckers are white and rubbery-looking. I hesitate, then lay my palm against the wall.

At last he subsides, and sinks to the bottom of the tank. He's pale pink now.

"You're home," I tell him.

I check the tank controls, then turn out the lights and go back to bed. In the darkness I lie awake and think of Venus, who was raised in a laboratory and never knew the open ocean. Who has no idea what a thing called a *sea* even is.

I go to the aquarium. It's just a few blocks from the apartment—we used to go there, from time to time.

I find my way through the dark underground galleries, past shoals of tiny silver fish and sharks that coast in eternal circles. Past the luminous jellyfish tanks and a horrible wolf eel and a display of tiny seahorses bouncing through weeds.

I find her coiled in the ceiling of her tank, embraced by coral.

For a long time I float in the darkness, looking up at her. She breathes softly, her mantle fluttering. Her skin is pallid, unconcerned. It takes me a couple of minutes to spot her eye, watching me back.

Her sign says she's *Octopus vulgaris*, the common octopus. It seems strange to me that she doesn't approach the glass, until I remember that she's just an animal. And that to her, I'm nothing but a blur of pinkish light.

I get home late, drop my briefcase on the chair by the door, and loosen my tie as I walk to the tank. Reed's lying on the bottom, his color mimicking the pinkish sand as if he's indifferent, or bored.

I tug my tie over my head and look at him. "Is everything okay?"

I don't expect him to do much, maybe just to blink a few times to let me know he's all right. But he gathers himself and climbs to the top of the tank. He fiddles with the lid, and then I watch his arms emerge from the water and curl like question marks over the wall. He hangs there, his arms coming up one by one to feel the air.

"Reed?" I feel something unfamiliar—a touch of wariness. "Are you okay?"

He extends one arm toward me, querulous. It drips onto the carpet. I step closer, and the arm extends still farther, until the tip brushes my jacket. It moves up and touches my throat, my chin, my cheek. It feels like a finger in a cold dish glove.

Reed adjusts his body and the arm grows a little longer, long enough to settle on my shoulder and pull. Octopuses learn with their arms, I remember. Their eyes are marvelous but they can't see past a few feet.

I swallow my nervousness and step toward the tank. Right up to the edge, so we're only separated by the crystal-clean acrylic. Reed's body is pressed softly against it, his mantle sagging because he's lifted himself half out of the water. The Spanish word for octopus, *pulpo*, surfaces in my mind.

Above my head, his arms uncoil in all directions, dripping cold water. They settle over my shoulders like the lead X-ray apron at the dentist's office. He moves his body, squeaking against the wall, until his eye is aligned with mine. His iris is golden, his pupil black and fathomless. His suckers pull at me in a hundred places, cold soul-kisses.

"Reed." I put my fingers against the wall, next to his eye. "What are you doing, honey?"

He smells of salt water, and very faintly of sweet sepsis. The tip of one arm settles against my face, then curves around my head. It tightens.

"Reed!" I pull my head away, and immediately all his arms lock onto me. My spine flares, my feet leave the ground. He has one arm around my chest, squeezing. Another snaking around my throat.

I realize that all of a sudden I'm seeing the water from above, that I'm up over the knocked-askew lid of the tank, and that in another second I'll be in. Into five cubic meters of freezing ocean water. With Venus.

My toe cracks into something, and the emergency bell starts to scream. Reed gives a massive shudder and drops me.

I scramble backward, gasping.

When I get up he's curled in a tiny, tight ball in the farthest corner of the tank. His eyes are closed. He's dark purple, a shade I've never seen him before.

I can't decide what's just happened. "Reed." I wipe water from my face. "What were you trying to do?"

He doesn't move. For a long moment I think he's not going to reply. Then he uncoils and hauls himself to the keyboard. I think of a scolded dog, crawling on its belly.

i forget

"You forget what you were trying to do?"

no

I wait.

i forget you He stops typing. There's a sudden constriction in my throat. "You forget me?"

no He types quickly, decisively, as if he's emphasizing this. *nnot you iforget you cant come*

"You forget I can't come where?"

in

I stand with my hand on my neck, staring at him.

you cant come inthesea

I linger in the shower, first to cry and then to shave. The skin of my throat is tender. When I wipe the steam from the mirror I see rough red circles garlanding my neck.

When we decided on the transplant, we knew there were things we couldn't predict. Taking Reed out of his body, his beautiful fucked-up broken body—how could we have known what that would do?

I thought I didn't care. I thought it was enough for me that he wouldn't be in pain anymore, that we could leave behind the catheters and ports and titanium screws, the radiation and the chemicals. The patches of shiny skin all over his body, over the parts they'd taken out, sunken like the hollow over a fresh grave. The same sunken look around his eyes, as time wore on.

When they told us it had taken his spine, we said okay, we understand. They wanted to do the excision right away, so we signed the papers for that. We were very adult, very responsible.

They checked Reed in and I picked up some junky magazines—we called them newspapers—from the gift shop. We lay shoulder to shoulder in his twin bed, a bed that wouldn't have fit both of us even a few months before. We read together until a nurse came in and told me to leave. I remember thinking it was too early, it wasn't even eight o'clock.

I went home alone. I closed the door behind me, put my keys in the bowl, hung my coat in the closet, and went into the living room. I curled into a ball on the floor, right about where the tank sits now. I covered my head with my arms and cried.

The surgery was a bust. But there was one more possibility, one get-out-of-jail-free card. It was crazy, it was experimental. There were all kinds of chances that it wouldn't work.

Of course we signed the papers. I would have signed anything. I would have signed my own life away, to stay with him another day.

I lie down on the couch with a glass of bourbon and when I wake up my mouth feels parched and vile. The glass is on the carpet, the stain almost dry. My head feels huge. My watch says it's four o'clock in the morning.

I look at the tank, first thing. When I see it's empty I feel a dull emotion—not surprise. A kind of thump, like a medicine ball dropped on dirt. The tank lid is knocked aside. I don't see any tracks on the carpet.

I turn on every light, search every room. I call him. I already know he won't come. I look anyway, quickly and methodically, ignoring the increasingly painful beat of blood inside my temples. At last I notice a damp blot at the base of the front door. It's unlocked. How could I not have noticed? I step into my shoes and run out.

I have to ask Binjamin, the night doorman, to help me look. For my pet, I tell him—Binjamin has no context, he's just a beautiful doorman. Mr. Levitt's pet is missing. Together, we scour the lobby until I see a grey-pink wad socked into a tiny space behind one potted palm. We scrape the pot to one side and I reach behind. Reed's skin feels dry and pimply and slack.

"I can take it," Binjamin offers, clearly horrified, clearly wanting nothing to do with this. Reed's arms keep slipping out of mine, his mantle overflows my hands like wet dough. I'm wearing rumpled, booze-scented clothes. I know how I look. Puffy, red-eyed, unshaven, clutching my horrible prize. But Binjamin has always been kind. He says, "I can take it, Mr. Levitt," from a safe distance, a step or two away. His face frozen, his eyes wide.

I tell him it's okay. If he can just push the elevator button for me. We stand waiting for it together, the three of us. It takes forever.

I don't know how I get Reed back into the apartment, back into the tank. He's dead weight, unmoving. How long since he walked out of the apartment, took the elevator down to the lobby floor, and pulled himself into that dark crevice? And what did he think he was doing? Penury, for the reddened circle around my neck? Or was he running away?

I pull a chair next to the tank and sit watching. His gills tremble. His siphon moves. After a long time, he opens his eyes.

"You're such a prick," I say. Then I can't stop crying.

I take a few days off work. I sleep, shower, potter around the house. I play music and cook. I'm careful, I pay attention. I notice all the tiny, singular details of our lives in this place.

On the third day I wipe down the kitchen counters, put the sponge in the dishwasher, and fold the dish towels. I pull a chair next to the tank and sit down.

"I've been thinking." I watch Reed for any sign that he's listening. He hasn't spoken since I brought him back from the lobby. A few times I've wondered if he's even himself anymore. If maybe he's just Venus now, if the eye that watches me sees nothing more than a faint pinkish blur. "I don't think this is working out."

His eyelid flutters faintly, then lifts. He raises his eyes an inch from his head.

"I think we're at the end of our rope. I think we need to try something else." I lean forward and put my fingers to the wall. "We said no leaving. Not unless we go together."

He regards me. Then he unrolls himself across the tank floor and puts the tips of two arms to the wall, matching my fingers.

"Okay," I say. I feel a sense of release, relief. Almost literally, a weight lifted. I laugh. "Okay, good."

I ask Binjamin to bring me a plastic paint bucket, a sturdy one with a good handle. The one he brings is clean, maybe unused. I don't ask him where he got it, I just pass him the envelope with his Christmas tip in it—early this year—and say thank you. He gives me a sideways look and goes.

It's a big bucket, but still a tight fit. Some of Reed's arms don't stay in. The important thing is that there's some salt water in there, enough to cover his gills. I turn down the heat, turn off the lights. Before we go, I shut off the recirculator pump in the tank. The silence that falls is strange and final.

We take the freight elevator to the garage. No point frightening Binjamin any more than we have to.

I drive. Obviously.

It's past midnight when we get to the beach, and the parking lot is empty except for a VW van and a couple of sedans. Couples necking, maybe, or the kind of sketchy midnight deeds that Reed and I used to know more about when we were younger men. A million years ago.

It's a struggle, carrying the bucket over the sand. I have to set him down, sit down, and take off my shoes. The sand is surprisingly cold. Reed lifts his eyes up over the edge of the bucket, toward the white blur of the surf.

At the water's edge, I tip the bucket onto its side and stand back. Reed emerges like a pink blossom and slides out on the retreating surf. I wade in after him. The water's icy, and for a moment I'm afraid. But I think of the apartment, silent and empty. I keep walking.

We met for the first time at a party, Reed says. He says I was wearing a blue cardigan and pressed khaki pants, standing alone in the hallway. I was reading the spines of the host's books, holding an undrunk gin and tonic in my hand. I have no memory of that party, no memory of being introduced by our mutual friend. I do remember the cardigan—I thought it masked my belly and made me look smart. Reed enlightened me on both points.

I remember meeting him months later at a late-night showing of *Chinese Ghost Story*, sitting next to him in a group of friends and thinking stupidly, hotly, of him the whole time. His long tanned face, his snaggle-toothed smile, the cords that appeared in his neck when he turned his head. The way he seemed to be looking at me, a way no man had ever done. As if he'd noticed me. As if he wanted me.

A wave hits me mid-belly and rocks me up onto the balls of my feet. This is the worst part, I tell myself. Stomach and chest are the hardest. I walk faster, surging forward despite my pounding heart, my locked and chattering jaw.

I'm twenty or thirty feet from shore now, not so far that I couldn't turn around if I wanted to. But I don't want to. It's an adventure, I tell myself. At this point in my life I should be grateful for one last excitement. And besides, it'll be over soon.

I keep walking until the bottom drops out from under my feet and then I dog-paddle helplessly. The waves are black swells in the darkness. I rise and fall with the current. My legs feel sluggish. My breath comes in short, yelping gasps.

I don't see Reed but I know he's close by. He'll be here in a minute. He won't leave me behind. Salt water slops into my mouth and nose.

Far off, someone shouts. I crane my head back to look. Someone is waving a flashlight at the water's edge. I start paddling harder, with more purpose, out into the heaving dark.

Virginia Woolf was no fool; she filled her pockets with rocks. I forgot that step and now I'm bobbing like a fat cork. I hear more shouting, and on the crest of a wave I look back to see more lights. And more than that, worse than that—someone else is in the water. I watch, disbelieving. Someone with a strong stroke is setting out from the beach. Someone else is charging in.

I try to stop paddling, to let myself sink. Water closes over my head, but when it covers my face I panic and thrash to the surface. My ears and sinuses are sluiced with salt. I can't do this without help. Where's Reed?

It's Venus, I think. She never gave a damn about me, and now she's gone, flown the coop and taken Reed with her. The bitch. At some point I've started to cry.

Something brushes my leg and I jerk instinctively away. There's another touch, a firm grasp around my knee. Others around my thigh, my belly. I'm filled with both panic and relief.

"Oh thank God," I say, even though I know he can't hear me. His arms wrap around my waist and chest, around my shoulders. One reaches up to touch my face. I try to stop kicking, to let go.

I think of him in the seat beside me at the movie theater, in the kitchen of our first apartment, in the doctor's office, with the sunny view out over the city, when they told us he was sick.

"Okay," I say. I'm afraid the swimmers will get here soon. "I'm ready, honey."

His grip tightens. For a second I can't breathe.

Then he lets go.

I tread water, waiting. Searching for him in the blackness. He'll come back, I know. He'll take me with him, wherever he goes. That's what we agreed on, that was the deal.

I'm still waiting when the first fearless rescuer finds me and grabs hold of me, to tow me back to shore.

About the Authors

Camille Alexa is a Canadian and American author currently living in the Pacific Northwest near volcanoes, forests, and ocean. Her genre-fluid fiction has appeared in *Ellery Queen's* and *Alfred Hitchcock's* Mystery Magazines, *Machine of Death*, and *Imaginarium 2012: The Best Canadian Speculative Writing*. Her award-nominated collection *PUSH OF THE SKY* earned a starred review in *Publishers Weekly* and was an official reading selection of Portland's Powell's Books SF Book Club. More at **camillealexa.com**.

Brenda Anderson lives in Adelaide, South Australia with her husband and two children. Her fiction has appeared in *Andromeda Spaceways Inflight Magazine, A cappella Zoo, Bards and Sages Quarterly* and *Punchnel's*.

T.E. Grau is a dark fiction author whose work has appeared in numerous anthologies, including *Tales of Jack the Ripper, The Best of The Horror Society 2013, Dead But Dreaming 2, The Aklonomicon, Urban Cthulhu: Nightmare Cities, Horror for the Holidays, Dark Fusions: Where Monsters Lurk*, and *Mark of the Beast*, among others; the print magazines *Dark Intent* and *LA Weekly*, and the electronic publications *Lovecraft eZine* and *Eschatology Journal*. In addition to fiction writing, he is an essayist and contributor to *The Teeming Brain, We Love Monsters, LORE, The Horrifically Horrifying Horror*

Blog, *Yog-Sothoth.com*, *Thomas Ligotti Online*, and the *Esoteric Order of Dagon Amateur Press Association* (edited by S. T. Joshi). In the editorial realm, he currently serves as Fiction Editor of *Strange Aeons* magazine. T.E. Grau currently lives in Los Angeles with his wife, daughter, and bunny named Cthulhu, and you can find him in the ether at *The Cosmicomicon* (**cosmicomicon.blogspot.com**).

Ives Hovanessian is a screenwriter and author of noir, uncanny and horror fiction. Her first screenplay, *Trendsetters*, was optioned by Colossal Entertainment. She is also a contributing columnist for *The Horrifically Horrifying Horror Blog* and the Editor of *Dark Intent Magazine* (White Cat Publications). She is currently working on her first novel, *Dog Will Hunt*, and *"I Am Death," Cried The Vulture*, a debut collection of short stories. She lives in Los Angeles with her husband and daughter.

Joe Jablonski writes out of Charlotte, NC. He has work published or forthcoming in a variety of markets including *Eschatology*, *Absent Willow Review*, *M-Brane SF*, *Short-Story.ME! Genre Fiction*, and *Liquid Imagination*. You can check out his blog at **jablonskijoe.blogspot.com**.

Jamie Lackey lives in Pittsburgh with her husband and their cat. Her fiction has been published by over a dozen different venues, including *The Living Dead 2*, *Beneath Ceaseless Skies*, and *Daily Science Fiction*, and she has appeared on the Best Horror of the Year Honorable Mention and Tangent Online Recommended Reading Lists. She reads slush for *Clarkesworld Magazine*, works as an assistant editor at *Electric Velocipede*, and helped edit the *Triangulation Annual Anthology* from 2008 to 2011. Her Kickstarter-funded short story collection, *One Revolution*, is available on Amazon.com. Find her online at **jamielackey.com**.

Claude Lalumière (**lostmyths.net/claude**) is the author of the collection *Objects of Worship* (CZP 2009) and the mosaic novella *The Door to Lost Pages* (CZP 2011). He has edited twelve anthologies in various genres, the latest of which is *Super Stories of Heroes & Villains* from Tachyon Publications. With Rupert Bottenberg, Claude is the co-creator of *Lost Myths* (**lostmyths.net**), which is an online archive of cryptomythology, a growing collection of pop artefacts, and a multimedia live show.

D. Thomas Minton resides with his wife and daughter on a little speck of land in the middle of the vast Pacific Ocean. When not writing, he works as marine biologist helping local communities conserve their coral reefs. His fiction has appeared in *Asimov's Science Fiction*, *Lightspeed Magazine*, *Daily Science Fiction*, and numerous other publications. His idle ramblings hold court at **dthomasminton.com** and would appreciate your visit.

Karen Munro's work has appeared or is forthcoming in *Strange Horizons*, *Luna Station Quarterly*, *Electric Spec*, and *The Again*. She completed her MFA in Fiction at the Iowa Writers' Workshop in 1999 and is at work on a novel about strange things.

Danna Staaf is a marine biologist, a science writer, a novelist, an artist, and an educator. She fell in love with octopuses at the age of ten, began to keep them as pets, and eventually conducted research on them and their fellow cephalopods. She holds a BA in Creative Studies from the University of California, Santa Barbara, and a PhD in Squid Babies from Stanford University. She lives in San Jose with her husband and two cats.

Elizabeth Twist is a speculative fiction writer who lives in Hamilton, Ontario. She holds a PhD in English Literature, which she earned by combing 400 year old medical manuals for evidence that syphilis and the plague influenced the plays of Shakespeare. Her short fiction has appeared in *Escape Clause: A Speculative Fiction Annual*, *Misfit Magazine*, and *One Buck Horror*. She is currently working on a novel-length alternative history of the Black Death involving vigilante nuns, shamanistic rebels, and necromantic prostitutes. Find her online at **elizabethtwist.com**.

Henry W. Ulrich is an unrepentant nerd, beard enthusiast, and cephalopod admirer who lives in the commonwealth of Pennsylvania. A graduate of Shippensburg University, he currently works at an academic publishing house, plays far too many tabletop roleplaying games when given the opportunity, and turns into an irritable ball of fuzz when poked.

About the Illustrator

Natasha Aldred is an illustrator based in West Yorkshire, England. Her illustration style consists of edgy themes, fluent ink marks and a strong aspect of texture, vibrant colours or strong tones which often hide the occasional naked lady or quirky face. She uses hand drawn marks to create her work and layers collage materials to create colour and texture to the pen work. She takes a lot of inspiration from narratives, alternative fashion and lifestyles, music, and photography. Visit her at at **natashaaldred.com**.

About the Editor

David Joseph Clarke is an independent filmmaker and media consultant, currently working within the broadcast industry and non-profit organisations both nationally and abroad. Originally from Germany, where he produced documentary content for television, David moved to the United States in 2007. There he began a career in the film industry, working as a producer and assistant director for various independent feature and short film projects in New England, USA, Australia, and Puerto Rico.

A fan of cephalopods since his youth, Suction Cup Dreams is his first published anthology project. David's greatest goal in life is to one day collaborate with an octopus on a revolutionary art project.

ACKNOWLEDGMENTS

Working on a project as vast and extensive as this book takes a lot of work and support from a wide range of people. I would like to personally thank each and every author who participated in writing stories for this book and everybody who believed in this anthology project. I would like to thank Aerica diPonzio, Thomas Nöla, Linda Ocasio, and Dara Roberts for their contributions during the decision-making process. Illustrator Natasha Aldred achieved amazing work bringing the stories to life, and Pelican Bishop who took time off on a trip to Hawai'i to help out with graphical elements as well. Special kudos go to Eleanor Luna for her expert proofreading skills and support.

More thanks go out to Timothy Deal of Shroud Publishing who hosted AnthoCon in New Hampshire, where I received lots of support for the project, and Tim Lieder of Dybbuk Press who was always a font of suggestions and ideas for making a better product.

I especially want to thank you for reading this book. supporting these great writers and authors, and for sharing the love of the octopus.

— David Joseph Clarke

89213808R00095

Made in the USA
San Bernardino, CA
21 September 2018